"Roddie's New Woodlot provid
could just as well be yours or n
traditional "How to Manage ..
but seeing the forest ecosystem as a whole: the soils, the plants, the wildlife, the people, and how they all interact within the community; a community which could be yours. A must read for anyone with a fondness for the Woods!"
— Doug Archibald, Regional Wildlife Biologist,
NS Dept. Natural Resources

"I loved Roddie and equally enjoyed Roddie II. It's great when you can be entertained while learning lots of good stuff about our natural world. It's a wonderfully easy read and a great educational source for anyone interested in nature."
— Don Cameron, RPF, Regional Forester, Information Officer, Canadian Institute of Forestry (NS Section)
NS Dept. of Natural Resources

"Your book has given me a whole new perspective of planet earth. For the most part, the complex interactions within the environment are taken for granted on a day-to-day basis. This book encourages us to stop, look, listen and think about the interdependence within our natural environment. Attempting to understand the "why" will go a long way in determining the "how"."
— Reg Conohan, Provincial Forest Supervisor
Eastern Forestry District, PEI

"If you don't need to read it for its educational value, then read it for its entertainment value." I thoroughly enjoyed the book.
— Clifton Sangster, CFT, Forest Technologist
North Inverness Forest Management Ltd., NS

RODDIE'S NEW WOODLOT

Lessons on Nature and
Ecological Woodlot Restoration

GIRVAN HARRISON

Copyright © 2007 by Girvan Harrison

All rights reserved. No part of this book may be reproduced or transmitted in any form or by any means, electronic or mechanical, including photocopying, recording, or an information storage and retrieval system without permission in writing from the publisher.

Published by
Earthwood Editions
2097 Route 102, Gagetown
New Brunswick, Canada
E5M 1K9

This is a work of creative non-fiction, names, characters and incidents are the product of the author's imagination and any resemblance to persons or places is entirely coincidental. However, Nature's functions, systems and processes are true according to current ecological understanding.

Library and Archives Canada Cataloguing in Publication

Harrison, Girvan, 1943 –
Roddie's new woodlot: lessons on nature and ecological woodlot restoration/Girvan Harrison

ISBN: 978-0-9686599-4-6
Ps 8615.A772R63 2007   C813'.6   C2007-904208-2

All illustrations by Ian Smith: Ian Smith Originals
Author's photo by Brian Rau: Brian Rau Photography
Printed in the United States of America
1. Woodlots – Management – Fiction. 2. Ecology – Fiction. I.Title.

To those who are learning or now realize, that Nature *isn't* just a vast resource warehouse whose sole purpose is to satisfy human wants. These people have come to see Nature as a wonderous, gigantic complexity of interlinking systems and processes that sustains life in *all* its forms - and are humbled by this knowledge.

ACKNOWLEDGEMENTS

Writing is, and must be, a solitary experience. So is reading. However, the writing process itself is usually supported by many others. This book is no exception.

I express my deep gratitude to the following for their valued discussions, advice, guidance and encouragement. Thanks to Doug Archibald, Bob Bancroft, Tom Boulter, Don Cameron, Kenny McGinn, David McDonald, Clifton Sangster, and Robert Whitney.

A special thanks to John Torunski. John has carefully reviewed this and my previous books and has always promptly provided valued comments.

Also, a special thanks to Heather Flinn who has cheerfully typed the seemingly endless revisions required to produce this and my other books.

And a sincere thanks to Bob Ross of Global Technology Systems Inc. A good friend to anyone such as myself; for my computer confusion is indeed impressive.

Thanks to my wife Marie, whose patience, support, and understanding has allowed me to spend the many hours necessary to put words on paper – and not feel too guilty.

However, even with all of the help from others, errors sometime creep into the text. If they did – they're my responsibility.

• LEGEND •

INTERMITTENT BROOK	→~
EXTRACTION ROAD	~~
TRAIL	- - - - -
FOXBROOK ROAD	▬▬▬
OLD CELLAR	▢
STAND BOUNDARY	— - - —
ROCK OUTCROP	♛
STONE FENCE	8⊙8⊙8
STAND NUMBER	①
SPRING	●

• not drawn to scale •

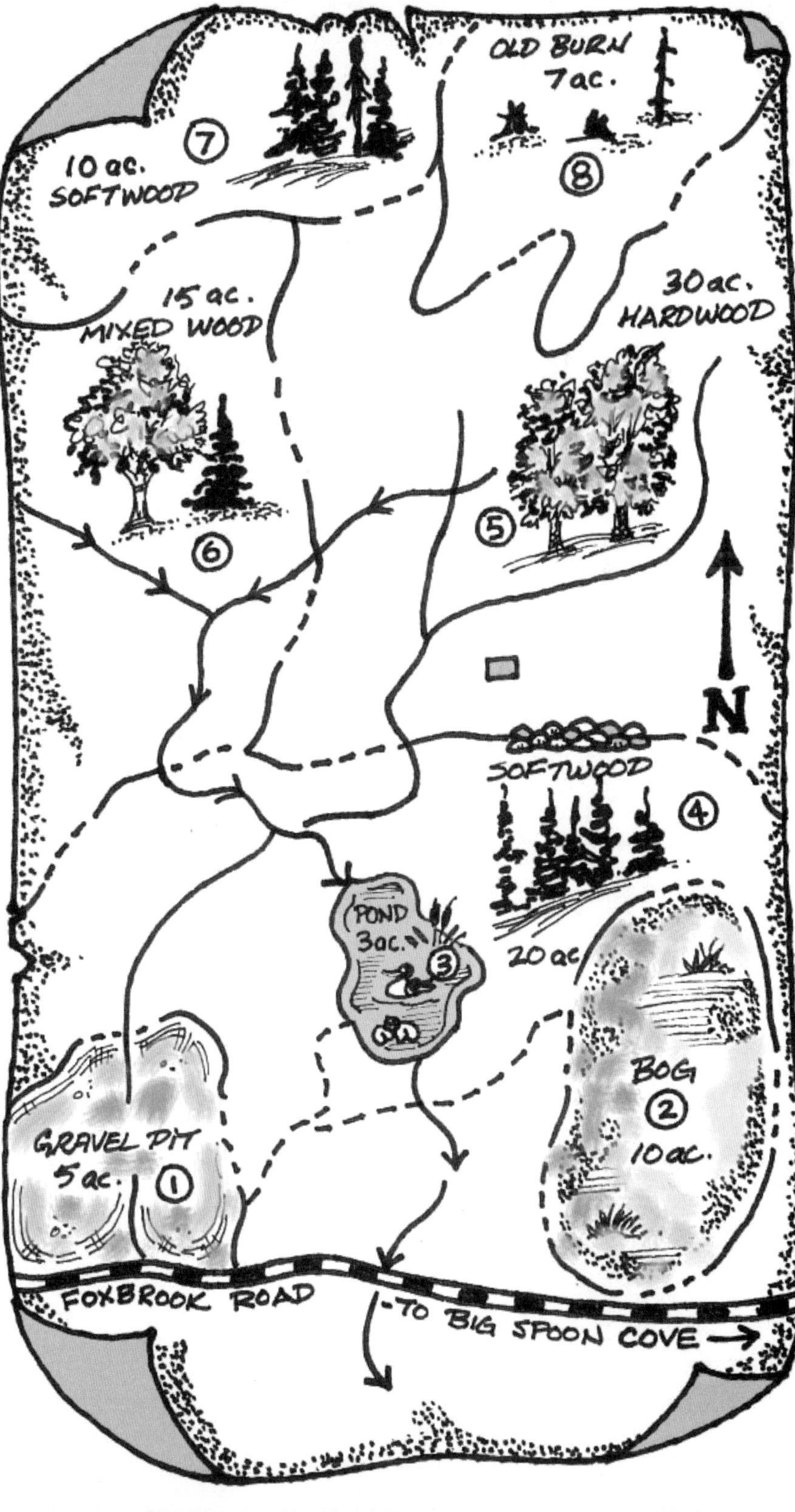
OLD BURN
7 ac.
⑦
10 ac.
SOFTWOOD
⑧
15 ac.
MIXED WOOD
30 ac.
HARDWOOD
⑥
⑤
N
SOFTWOOD
④
POND
3 ac.
③
20 ac.
BOG
②
10 ac.
GRAVEL PIT
5 ac.
①
FOXBROOK ROAD
TO BIG SPOON COVE

SOMETHING TO PONDER

*The forest is a peculiar organism of unlimited kindness
and benevolence that makes no demands for its sustenance
and extends generously the products of its life activity;
it provides protection to all beings, offering shade even
to the axe man who destroys it.*
Gautma Buddha
Circa 525 B.C.

*It is well to remember that there are no new forests
to be found. All are known. From here to eternity
we must do with what we have.*
Herbert Lash
1966

CONTENTS

ACKNOWLEDGEMENTS............................... vii
SOMETHING TO PONDER............................... x
FOREWORD xiii
AUTHOR'S NOTE xv

A SATURDAY AFTERNOON AT RODDIE'S CAMP........... 3
RODDIE'S OLD GRAVEL PIT 17
THE SCHOOL VISIT 33
BARBERS, BLUES, BATS AND RATS 47
PONDS, BOGS AND OTHER THINGS WET 61
AN IDEALIST, A CYNIC, OR A REALIST? 77
MUSINGS WHILE WALKING WITH A HERMIT........... 89
THE PAST, THE PRESENT, AND THE FUTURE........... 101
LETTERS, E-MAILS,
    PHONE CALLS, AND CONVERSATIONS 117
BARBEQUES, BANTER, AND BELIEFS 127
THE WATER, WILDLIFE, AND WOOD WALKABOUT...... 149
EPILOGUE... 171
APPENDIX A:
    IDENTIFICATION OF SITE FACTORS 172
APPENDIX B:
    SOIL TEXTUREASSESSMENT GUIDE 174
APPENDIX C:
    SPECIES/SITE SELECTION PLANTING KEY........ 176
APPENDIX D:
    DESIRABLE STOCKING AFTER THINNING 179

GLOSSARY... 181

FOREWORD

Treat the Earth well: it was not given to you by your parents, it is loaned to you by your children. In the early years of this, the 21st century, with a human population exceeding 6.5 billion it is time we considered this adage and what we will give back to our children.

Increasingly we are becoming an urban population which depends upon an ever-dwindling supply of resources from an ever-shrinking productive land base. As we become more urbanized we loose touch with the land and an understanding, a feeling, for how the earth`s natural systems work.

The forest is a dynamic ecosystem capable of adapting to change over time. The operative word is *time*, as forest time is measured in centuries and not decades, as is human time.

The development of soils, the hydrologic cycle, the miracle of photosynthesis, the cycling of nutrients, the evolution and interactions of flora and fauna are all workings of a living, functioning, evolving forest.

Often that which is most difficult to see is right in front of you and this could not be more obvious then when one begins to carefully observe, study and understand the forest around us. Riparian zones, wetlands, dead trees, cavity trees, fungi, forest succession, old growth, aesthetics, spirituality; these are all parts and values of a forest system which one learns to appreciate with time.

In "Roddie's New Woodlot" Girvan Harrison provides us with an insight into a living forest with sound thoughts and lessons on planning and practicing ecological woodlot management......and although the understanding may take some time, it is as John Alex so often says, "In just two days tomorrow will be yesterday" and I would thus suggest that it is high time we got on with it!

—Doug Archibald
Wildlife Biologist

AUTHOR'S NOTE

Many, perhaps even most of us, don't ever think about Nature. That is until something happens. Something that affects humans. Maybe it's a flood, wildfire, or hurricane that seriously impacts some people. Or, it could be a prolonged hot spell, cold spell, rainy spell, snowy spell, or dry spell. We're not picky about what we grumble about.

However, few humans seem to understand how Nature works – its timing chain, fuel, gears and cogs, indeed the very nuts and bolts of an intricate machine that makes life possible on the "third rock" from the sun. This book will examine, and hopefully explain, some of these systems and processes as they pertain to a particular woodlot in Nova Scotia. A woodlot owned by an opinionated curmudgeon by the name of Roddie MacInnis.

You'll also meet many other characters who live in the small fishing village of Big Spoon Cove. Characters as diverse as Glory Be, Roddie's sister; John Alex, the neighbour who lives to tease Roddie; Stanley Farquar, the retired banker; and many more. Those of you that have read either of my two previous books (Out Roddie's Way, and Out Roddie's Way – revised second edition) will be familiar with some of the characters. However, this book takes a totally different approach to the topic of woodlot management.

Throughout the book we'll examine and discuss some of the "wows" and "whys" of Nature, and how this understanding can be applied to assure the sustainability of the many forest values found in woodlots. Woodlots that have been, are being, and will be, impacted by natural and human-caused disturbances.

My intent is not to criticize professional groups for what was done in the past, but rather to point out that our expanding knowledge must result in things being done differently in the future. Although humour is used to convey the messages, I urge you to ponder upon the lessons. Lessons that identify and explain Nature's "gears and cogs." But lessons that are nothing short of miraculous, because we'll begin with four basic ingredients: rock, sunlight, air, and water. We'll then explore the natural systems and processes that combine these four ingredients into the miracle of Roddie's New Woodlot.

In March, Roddie purchased this one-hundred acre woodlot from a so-called harvesting contractor called Johnny Cutrone (known behind his back as Johnny Cut An' Run). The woodlot was, to use Roddie's expression, "skinned alive." Roddie didn't have to pay much for the lot. We'll use this lot as our study area to both explore how Nature functions, and to discuss long-term strategies for restoring his woodlot. So sit back and prepare to meet some interesting characters who live in an around Big Spoon Cove. Characters who, each in their own way, play a part in Roddie's New Woodlot.

RODDIE'S NEW WOODLOT

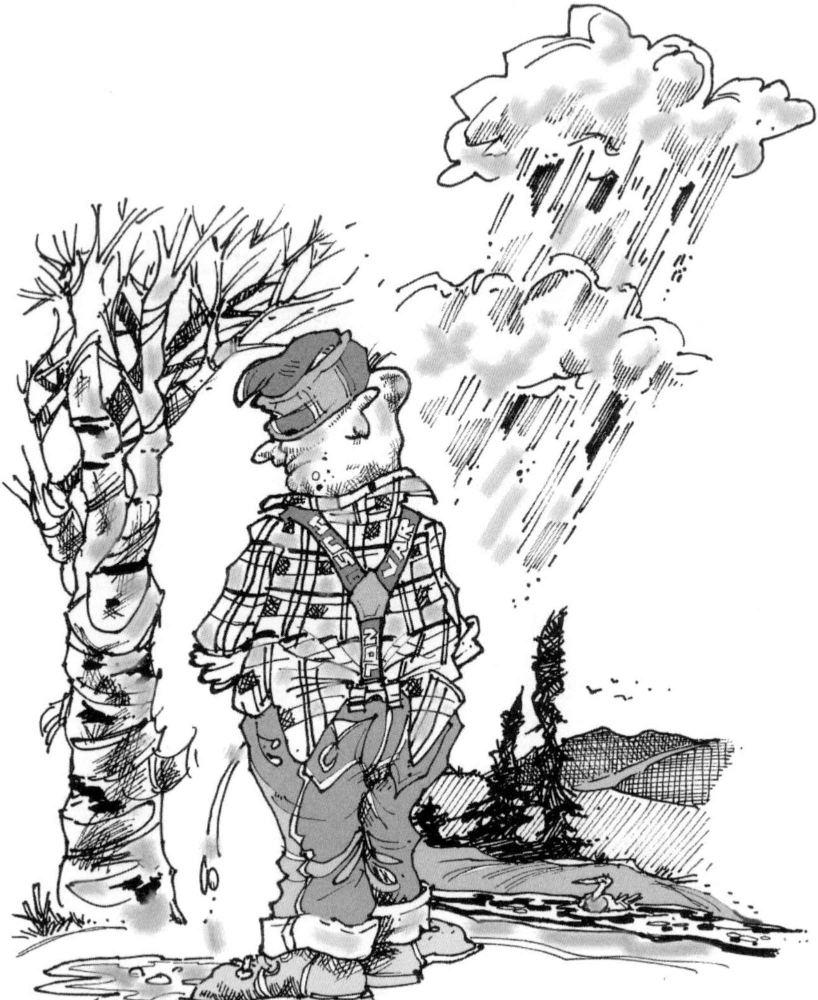

A SATURDAY AFTERNOON AT RODDIE'S CAMP

> *Ideal conversation must be an exchange*
> *of thought, and not, as many of those who*
> *worry most about their shortcomings believe,*
> *an eloquent exhibition of wit or oratory.*
> - Emily Post

As I drove over to Roddie's camp the sky was the colour of a Halifax sidewalk and the steady whap, whap, whap of the windshield wipers set me to musing upon my many trips to his camp. I thought about the night that I and others got stormed in at the camp.[*1] Gosh, although I see Roddie weekly, if not daily, it's been four years since that night I spent there. Time sure does fly. A quote from someone – I couldn't remember who, came to mind, "Time is change; we measure its passing by how much things alter."

My mind drifted back to that stormy night. Let's see, I thought, there was Roddie, his wife Dr. Jean, his sister Glory Be, Stanley

---

1 * See *OUT RODDIE'S WAY – Beauty Is In The Eye*

Farquhar, Dr. Dave Simpson, Gerald Fitzgerald, and the monk Brother Thomas. I couldn't remember if John Alex was there or not.

The contractor, Gerald Fitzgerald was now dead; killed when a split-wheel rim struck him in the face while he was inflating a truck tire. Dave Simpson was now working in British Columbia. Stanley had lost all his hair, and Brother Thomas was still living in his hermitage in the woods behind the monastery over in New Harbour. I made a mental note to drop over and see him again as I turned into Roddie's woods road.

I parked my truck and ran quickly though the driving rain to the camp. Roddie and John Alex were sitting in rocking chairs, a steaming tin mug in their hands, and a look of contentment on their faces as the rain pounded on the metal roof.

"Uncommonly fine large day, what!" cried Roddie. John Alex nodded and mumbled, "Think this rain'll ever stop, eh? Martha always says thet if'n ya kin see the barn it's goin' ta rain an' if'n you can't see it, it's aready rainin.' April showers brings dreary hours, eh?"

"Be a long wet spell, if it don't stop rainin'," smiled Roddie. "Pour yerself a good cup a Morses' bulk tea there young fella, an' draw up a chair. We wass jest talkin' 'bout the rain an' I gut a question fer ya.

"Watch thet kettle handle, it's some hot. I'm burnin' beech taday."

I sat and we made small talk about who's doing what to whom in the village. Finally, Roddie winked at John Alex and said to me, "The other mornin' some yahoo on the CBC radio said thet when yer drinkin' a glass a water there's a chance thet yer drinkin' a molecule er two a water from Napoleon's, er Churchill's, er Hitler's bladder. Did ya effer hear sech foolishness in all yer life?"

John Alex scratched one of his double chins and nodded sagely. "Yep, I hears thet some a them bureaucats only gut two brain cells thet communicates by e-mail oncest a day; walkin' arguments fer birth control, eh?"

"Yiss, yiss," said Roddie, not to be outdone, "Prob'ly gut sailboat fuel fer brains. What doess ya think young fella?"

"I hate to get dragged into this, but the CBC guy is correct. We drink recycled water and breath recycled air," I answered.

"Jesus, Mary an' Joseph, an' the little donkey too, are ya serious? A blind man racin' by on a gallopin' horse can see thet can't be so. Are ya one a them idjits too? Always kinda suspected thet ya wass a closet idjit."

"Well, you've often called me worse, but if you give me a chance I'll explain why the guy is right."

Roddie nodded, slurped some tea, wiped his moustache with a swipe of his hand, and sat ahead in his chair. John Alex leaned over to one side and had a methane moment. It sounded like someone stepped on a duck.

"Ok, to begin, the Earth is just a big spaceship. Gravity prevents anything from leaving its surface. Do you guys agree?"

"Guesses so, eh?" said John Alex, as he sniffed the air with obvious satisfaction.

"Yiss, yiss, we can't pull over an' take on supplies from anawhere else I guesses – so?"

"So, Nature has to recycle water, air, energy and other things and has systems to do just that."

"Wal, fer instance, how doess water git recycled then? Listen ta it beatin' on the roof like a gang a woodpeckers in passin' gear."

"Let's say that you have a bucket full of water. The water in this bucket represents all of the water on Earth. This includes not only surface water, but underground water, and water in the air surrounding the Earth. In short, every drop of water is contained in this huge bucket. Ok?"

"Yiss, yiss, be quite a bucket though," replied Roddie.

John Alex wriggled uncomfortably in his rocking chair. "I needs a pillow, me asteroids are actin' up somethin' awful."

"John Alex ain't gut much hay in hiss loft, one day hiss mind jest kinda wandered off an' ain't been seen since," chuckled Roddie. "Now, ya wass sayin'?"

"Now, suppose a hole suddenly appears in the bottom of our bucket and it slowly begins to drip-drip-drip-drip. Eventually all the water would be gone. If the water in the leaking bucket is to remain at a constant level, the volume of water that leaks out must somehow be replaced. Nature has a way of doing this, and it's called the hydrologic cycle. There are five interconnecting processes that happen; condensation, precipitation, infiltration, runoff, and evaportranspiration.

"John Alex, when you take a bottle of cold beer out of the refrigerator and let it sit for a while in a warm kitchen what happens?"

"Ah…I gits thirsty, eh?"

"Probably, but that's not the answer I was looking for. The beer bottle sweats. This happens because there's water vapor in the air in the kitchen and as the warm, vapor-laden air comes in contact with the cold bottle, water droplets form."

"Yiss, yiss, jest like dew on the grass in the mornin'," said Roddie.

"Right, now let's look at the big picture. Water is pretty neat stuff. Think about it. A water molecule, H_2O, consists of two atoms of hydrogen and one oxygen atom. These are both gases, yet when they combine they can remain as a gas, or become a liquid, or even a solid. And this allows water to adapt to the different conditions on Earth – from the equator to the North and South Poles.

"Just like John Alex's beer bottle sweating in a warm room, condensation happens in the atmosphere when the temperature of the Earth or the air changes. When air cools enough, water vapor condenses on particles that are floating in the air and clouds form.

"High and low atmospheric pressures cause winds which blow

these clouds across the landscape thus spreading the water vapor. Eventually, the clouds can't hold any more moisture and the Earth gets the water back in precipitation – rain, sleet, hail or snow."

"But gettin' back ta Churchill an' the boys' bladders, are ya sayin' thet when Churchill, for instance peed on a pansy out behind his War Cabinet, thet some a it went up inta the air?"

"Fer modesty's sake he should a gone inta the War Cabinet an' shut the door," observed John Alex.

It struck me funny. "Yes, some molecules probably did go directly into the air, but Churchill's War Cabinet wasn't a structure like a privy. It consisted of a group of his war advisors."

"Yiss, yiss an' called the Privy Council," smirked Roddie.

John Alex nodded solemnly. " I gutta go out ta the privy council an' send some bladder molecules up ta the wife's ugly sister in Bathurst. I'm jest becomin' like me father when he wass old, a serial urinator, eh."

"We'll not wait fer him. So, what happened ta the rest a Churchill's pee?"

"Next, three things happened at the same time. Some of the urine seeped into the ground. But if it was a sunny day, some evaporated, thus changing into a vapour which floated up in the warm air to become condensed back into water droplets. And some of the urine became runoff, which stays on the surface and, just like your brook, flowed into a lake or the ocean from where it too eventually evaporated, condensed and fell as precipitation."

"Must a had ta pee awful bad ta generate thet much," chuckled Roddie.

Just then John Alex returned and trundled over and sat down.

"How's the weather out now?" asked Roddie.

John Alex, who had a wet streak running down the left leg of his blue jeans replied, "Ya might say, it's pissin' down rain, eh!" This was followed by a blink, chuckle, wheeze, and ended with a trouser cough that sounded like someone starting a Harley.

Roddie peered at the wet streak, "I sees thet yer bucket wass leakin' too."

"Yea, Jimmie kinda gut away on me," replied John Alex. "I thought thet he wass out but the rain probably discouraged him, eh!"

"Ya said the last one was transportation?" asked Roddie.

"No, I said it was evapotranspiration, which happens when water evaporates from the ground or is given off by plants and trees. Many people don't realize that when plants and trees take in water through their roots, pass it up through the stem, and then out through the leaves that this actually purifies the water. I remember reading somewhere that about 93% of the water on Earth is in the oceans and that this water is toxic to many plants, animals, and of course, to all humans. So fresh drinkable water isn't an unlimited resource."

"Wal, wal," said Roddie. "I guesses the CBC yahoo wasn't so daft. Jin Alek, the heat from the stove iss turnin' thet wet streak on yer pants inta a vapor. Guess thet vapor'll hev ta pass through a good many plants ta git thet smell outta it."

"Tain't mine yer smellin' ya ambulatory geriatric. It's Churchill's."

"By the way," said Roddie, " I invited thet new wildlife biologist ta drop in fer lunch so's I'd better heat up the beans thet Jean made fer us last night. I suppose ya knows him?"

"Yep, real good guy." Frugal MacDougall (his first name was Fruellen), took Rusty McGee's job as district wildlife biologist two weeks ago when Rusty was transferred to Kentville.

Frugal fit right into our office. He's a good biologist and a tireless worker, and, although noticeably shy, he seemed to lose his shyness when talking about animals, their habits, and habitats. I knew that Roddie, John Alex, and myself were in for a good afternoon.

While Roddie put more wood in the stove and then placed the big pot of beans on it to warm up, John Alex turned to me and said,

"Somethin' thet I wass wonderin' 'bout when I wass peein' all over me pant leg wass, why iss the ocean salty, but not the rivers? How doess this happen anaway?"

"Good question. I'll answer it by first saying that contrary to what most people think there's a mixture of many chemicals and salts dissolved in ocean water, so it's important to understand that it's only about 85% sodium chloride, the salt that we put on food. But this 85% makes the ocean salty. However, there are other chemical elements in the water such as calcium, sulphate, magnesium, potassium, and many more.

"The ocean's salty for two reasons. First, normal rainfall is slightly acidic and over a long time has gradually dissolved minerals from igneous and other rock types, and these mineral-laden waters have eventually been washed into the ocean. This is called 'weathering'; and we'll talk more about this process some day. Thus, over hundreds of millions of years, the percentage of saltiness or 'saline content' has become greater.

"Salts also become more concentrated in ocean waters because of evaporation. Heat from the sun vaporizes pure water back into the atmosphere leaving the salts behind. In this way the oceans also gradually become more salty.

"However, as in insect, fish, bird, and mammal populations; or even soil acidity, Nature has a system of checks and balances. This ensures that the water doesn't become too salty."

Just then there was a loud stamping of boots on the deck and a knock on the door.

"Come in, yer now out," hollered Roddie.

The door opened, and Frugal entered. He was greeted by a "Hi Frugal;" a "How ya gettin' on, eh;" and by, "An uncommonly fine large day, what?"

Frugal entered and bent down to remove his boots.

"What're ya doin? Leave them boots on, yer in me camp, not me house!"

A red-faced Frugal straightened up. Frugal is about 5' 8", thin, sports a salt and pepper beard, and usually has a constant twinkle in his eyes. And I'm told that he hasn't been seen in public since the second grade without a vest.

He stepped over to the table, pulled out a chair and sat. "Hi guys, great day for ducks."

"Yiss, yiss, lots a rain. I'm jest heatin' up the beans fer lunch. Doess ya drink tea er coffee?"

"Tea."

"The oracle over there iss jest tellin' us 'bout why the oceans iss salty. Prob'ly only knows the names a six colours, so take what he says with a grain a salt."

"Yes, I replied, but I wanted to point out that the Sargasso Sea is saltier than some other ocean waters. I know why it is, but I don't know the interesting story about eels. I need your help here Frugal."

"Stop the jeesless bus eh! 'Fore we gets off on thet, finish tellin' me 'bout why er how Nature keeps the oceans from becomin' even saltier," said a now distinctly Pamper-smelling, wet-legged John Alex. I hoped that Frugal wouldn't think that it was me.

"Oh yes, where was I? Yes, ok. There are three main ways that the salinity in ocean waters is balanced. First by precipitation and the discharge of fresh waters from rivers. Rivers only contain about 16 per cent salt. Second, by the fact that the elements in sea water eventually combine to form insoluble compounds called chemical precipitates that sink to the bottom and then become a part of the ocean floor. And third, because of biological organisms such as plants and animals. But before I continue, I don't know of any biological process that removes sodium from sea water. Do you know of any Frugal?"

"No, none that I'm aware of."

"Me neither, but calcium is extracted from the water by barnacles, mussels, clams, oysters, shrimp, crabs and lobsters to build their shells and skeletons; and coral reefs are made from calcium carbonate when excess amounts of calcium are precipitated out of sea water and drop to the ocean floor. The basic salt content however, appears to be balanced by temperature, from wide-spread circulation by global ocean currents, plus by the inflow of vast quantities of fresh water from both rivers, rain, and snow."

"Come an' git it, er I'll feed it ta the pigs."

We all took a place at the table.

"We'll ast our new friend Frugal ta please say grace," announced Roddie.

A red-faced Frugal bowed his head, and said:

"Lord, please bless this food to
nourish our bodies and minds as we seek
Your guidance in our quest to
understand Your many wonderous creations.
We do this in Jesus' name.
Amen."

Roddie and John Alex eyed each other and subtlety nodded. Frugal had apparently passed a test.

After we did the dishes, cleaned up, and John Alex went out to probably pee on his right pant leg, we sat in the rocking chairs. Roddie lit his pipe, and we settled in to a good camp talk.

Rain beat on the roof. It streamed down the windows. The camp was cosy. The tea was great.

"When I wass making' dinner ya mentioned the Sargasso Sea an' said somethin' 'bout wantin' Frugal's help 'bout eels. Why don't ya help thiss fella out Frugal? Everybody in Big Spoon Cove knows thet he's 'bout a haff a bubble off plumb. Needs all the help he kin git."

Just then, the door slammed and John Alex clomped over to his chair. He turned to Frugal, "Still pissin' down rain eh! Ya prob'ly don't haff a clue what thet *really* means, eh?"

Naturally Frugal didn't know what John Alex was referring to, but Roddie did. "Yiss, yiss, still rainin', an' I sees thet ya rewatered yer leg. Ya'll haff ta tie a rope ta thet thing so's ya kin tow it all the way out."

John Alex chuckled. "A rollin' wheel gathers no moss, eh? What wass we talkin' 'bout anaway?"

"Frugal," I said, "before you got here, we were talking about why the oceans are salty. I happened to mention the Sargasso Sea and eels but, no pun intended, I was getting into water that's over my head. Can you tell us the story on the eels?"

"Sure. The Sargasso Sea is a very salty body of water located in the middle of the North Atlantic Ocean. The Sea is a unique area. It's named after a type of seaweed called Sargassum that floats in large amounts on the surface. Now, although found in the middle of an ocean, it's called a sea because it's actually surrounded by four ocean currents. On the north by the North Atlantic Current, south by the North Atlantic Equatorial Current, east by the Canary Current and west by the Gulf Stream."

"How big iss it anaway?" asked Roddie.

"Well, I can't give you the exact dimensions, but it's something like 1 000 kilometres (621 miles) wide by about 3 000 kilometres (1864 miles) long."

"An' the eels?" asked John Alex.

"Ah, yes, the eels. The Sargasso Sea is where both the European and American eels are born. The larvae of both species hatch there and migrate either to Europe or to the east coast of North America. And the extraordinary thing is that the eels eventually return to the Sargasso to lay their eggs."

"So there are actually only two eel species? How do they differ?" I asked.

"Two species in the Sargasso Sea. They differ in biochemical markers and their number of vertebra. The European eel has 110 to 119 while the American eel has 103 to 110. However, having said that, both species look similar at a quick glance. There's another eel species found in the Pacific Ocean called the Japanese eel."

"You said that the eggs hatch into larvae in the Sargasso Sea. What happens then?" I asked.

Frugal replied, "Let's take the European eel as an example. The eel larvae is swept along by the Gulf Stream current. About three years later it reaches England. It's now about 45 mm long and, because it's transparent, it's called a glass eel. The glass eel then migrates up rivers, up small English creeks, or even snakes its way through wet grass to reach isolated inland ponds.

"Now in fresh water, transparent glass eels begin to get colour and are now called elvers. They live in this fresh water for 12 or 14 years, reaching a length of 60 to 80 centimetres (24 to 31 inches). They've gradually taken on a yellow color and so are then known as yellow eels.

"Then the interesting thing happens. In July, the mature eels head back to the ocean. They migrate from ponds, often crossing long distances over land, go down creeks to rivers – and finally reach the ocean. Here they begin their epic journey of up to 6 000 km (3,728 miles) to return to the Sargasso Sea to spawn. Their bodies change. Magically their gut dissolves. This means that they must make the journey on their own stored body energy. Their eyes also change. They become larger so that they can see in the darker ocean waters. These changed eels are now called silver eels."

"Thet's a long trip," said Roddie. "How long doess it take anaway?"

"Well," said Frugal, "I guess it depends. They swim about 15 kilometres (9.3 miles) each day, so I guess if you do the math it would take about a half a year for them to reach the spawning area."

"Issn't thet somethin'. "

I said, "Frugal, I've recently re-read Farley Mowatt's S*ea of Slaughter* and have to ask about the state of the eel population. Is it good, declining, or what? It seems to me that most natural resources are in trouble because of human over-consumption."

At this time poor John Alex broke wind and said, "Humph! Must be a turd beepin' fer the right a way, eh?"

Roddie just shook his head. He nodded towards John Alex and said, "A lesser lad than Frugal might a been staggered by yer fartin' and burpin' Jin Alex. Try an' keep both holes in yer little round body shut so's we kin learn somethin'."

John Alex chuckled. "Ass me mother useta say, a fartin' horse will neffer tire an' a fartin' mans the man ta fire, eh."

Frugal sat ahead in his chair and stroked his beard. "That's certainly a good question. I don't know if we're overharvesting a healthy eel population or not. Eels are a popular dish for many people and cultures. I recently read that in Europe 25 million kilograms of European eels are consumed yearly, while each year the Japanese eat more than 100 million kilograms. But, since 1997, the European demand for eels can't be met. However, all is not well in the eel's world. Since the early 1980s eel populations have declined because of a parasitic nematode. This parasite, which is now in American, European, and Japanese eels, hampers the eel's swim bladder ability to function properly. Picture it. A poor eel is on a long ocean voyage relying only upon its stored energy, and now its hydrostatic ability is damaged."

"I always figgered thet eels wass jest water snakes," said Roddie.

"Yep, me too," said John Alex as he inspected something crumbly he'd found in his ear. "Ain't they?"

"Well, many people also think that," said Frugal. "But they're certainly not snakes. They're fish, and this has been proven by their gonads."

"Ah...gonads? asked John Alex.

"Ovaries an' testicles Jin Alek, surely ya knows what they are!" growled Roddie.

"I knows what they are ya dumb old twat, but I neffer effer saw a fish swimmin' along with his balls hangin' out fer all the world ta see, eh?"

"The sexual organs are different in fish than in mammals John Alex," said Frugal.

"That's me point, eh. A watched clock neffer boils. Now, I thinks I'll head fer home. Martha's makin' a Jigg's dinner fer supper an' it's hard ta beat a feed a corned beef an' cabbage with the odd piece a carrot an' turnip throwed in."

After John Alex left we sat and rocked and talked for a while. The day's heavy rain was now reduced to a Scotch mist. The three of us then left, to hopefully return another day.

As I drove home the sun broke through the clouds. Beautiful! I then got to thinking about our sessions at Roddie's camp. Good company, having good food, good conversation, and good fun. Then a thought struck me, and I laughted out loud. I sure wouldn't want to be poor Martha tonight. Imagine! Under the sheets with John Alex – and him loaded down with baked wind pills, cabbage, and turnip that would all no doubt all be, "beepin' fer the right a way."

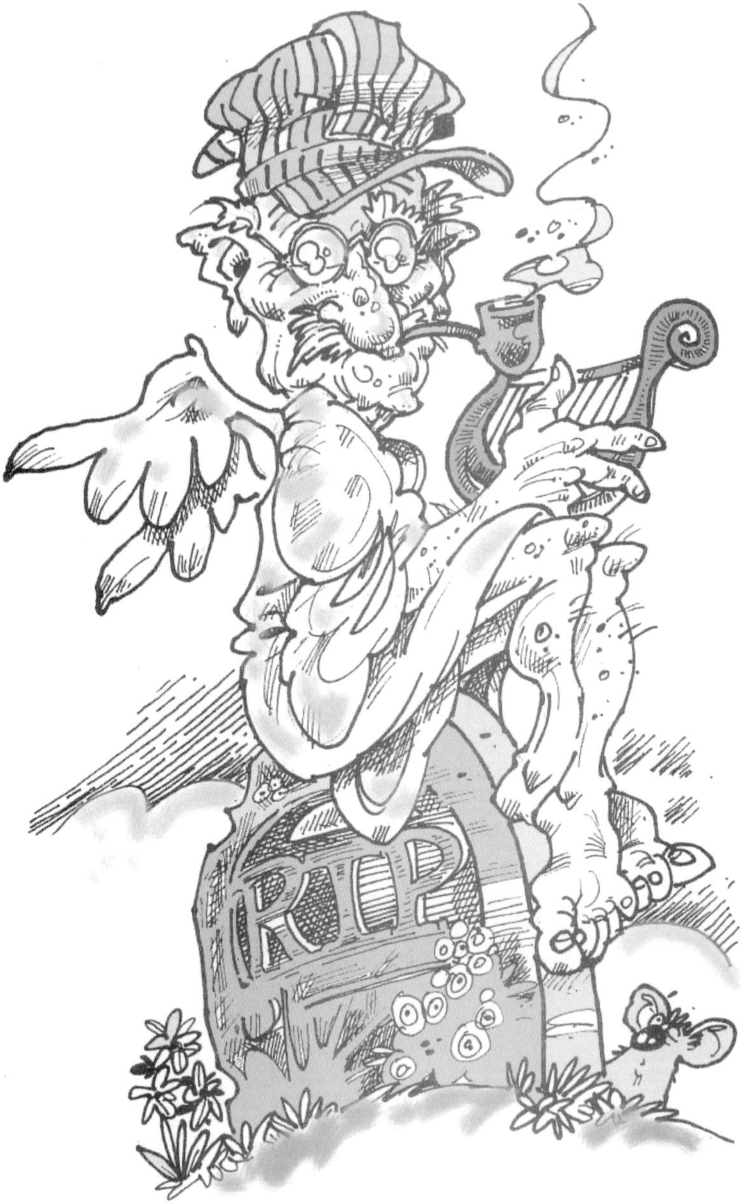
RIP

RODDIE'S OLD GRAVEL PIT

*Know a grain of sand completely and you
know the Universe in its entirety.*
- Ancient Proverb

It was 7:30 in the morning on May 2, when I got in my truck to head out to Roddie's new woodlot. A warm sunny morning, I drove through Big Spoon Cove with my window down; spring smells laced with a salty tang filled the cab.

As I turned in to the old gravel pit I could see Roddie and John Alex standing in the center of the pit tossing stones at an old oil can.

Competing again I thought. These two were always testing each other – from plowing the straightest furrow to throwing the best insult. They often remind me of two roosters in a hen house flapping their wings. But they were the very best of lifelong friends.

The reason for this visit resulted from something that I said yesterday. Roddie and his son, Roddie Too, were in my office, and during our conversation I happened to make a comment on the value of rocks. At the time, Roddie looked at me as though I had enough sawdust between my ears to bed a horse. He didn't say anything, but apparently a seed had been sown, for he phoned me later and asked me to meet him at his pit the next morning. And so, here we were.

As I walked over to them, Roddie's stone clanged into the can and sent it rolling.

"There ya go ya gommice. Try an' beat thet!"

"Pog mo thoin ya geriatric old fart," said John Alex. He turned and said to me, "Thinks thet he's the biggest cheeze on the village's pizza, eh?"

Roddie just dilated his nostrils, and said nothing.

I picked up a sandstone rock. "This is where it all begins," I said. They both looked at me rather vacantly and each bent down and picked up a rock. Roddie had a piece of granite, John Alex, a small piece of slate.

"What we each hold in our hand is the beginning and end of a miracle," I said.

"I imagine yer goin' ta explain, eh?" said John Alex.

"Yiss, yiss," said Roddie, "git on with it but ya don't have ta start when the Earth cooled!"

I went on to explain that although we each held a hard solid rock that, if you examined them through a high enough powered microscope, you would see that they were made up of molecules. That molecules were made up of atoms which consisted of a nucleus surrounded by electrons, and that at this submicroscopic level everything is moving, changing and vibrating.

"Now boys, the fascinating thing about atoms, is that at the atomic level, the electrons are separated from the nucleus by, at that scale, a vast distance. If, for example, a typical nucleus was scaled up to the size of a baseball, the diameter of the atom would be greater than two city blocks."

They looked at me as though my ladder was a couple of rungs short.

"Humph!' said Roddie. "Sounds like eau de equine ta me!"

I was puzzled until John Alex explained that this translated to "horse pee." I guess Roddie wanted a more practical explanation.

"Simple enough ta me though," said John Alex, "it's twice as long as half of it, eh?"

I had no idea what he was talking about! However, I carried on by saying that various types of rock have different fertility values. For example, the rocks that John Alex and I hold have a higher fertility value than Roddie's granite rock. That, in short, rocks were packages of mineral elements which are waiting to be released.

"Ya mean thet I've been pickin' and haulin' fist-sized packages an' even suitcases full a elements from my garden an' fields every spring?" asked Roddie, his eyes like two alarm clocks.

John Alex just stood there like an inukshuk and had a rather precarious-sounding methane moment.

"Ah…no," I answered, moving upwind from the smell of landfill and looking up expecting a descending flock of seagulls. Anyhow, I persisted and told the boys that yes, the stones and rocks did indeed contain elements such as calcium, potassium, iron and phosphorus, but that these elements were locked within the rock until they were released by a process called 'weathering'. Roddie was just removing rocks that had been brought to the surface by his plowing and by frost action, that were then interfering with him cultivating his fields and garden.

"What doess ya mean *weatherin'*, eh?" asked Chanel Number Five.

Roddie also looked at me expectantly.

"Well," I said, "perhaps we better start by looking at the Earth itself."

"Yiss, yiss. I knew ya'd eventually git back ta the coolin' bit," said Roddie.

I ignored him. "Picture an egg. You have the shell, the albumen, and the yoke. The shell can be compared to the Earth's crust which makes up 0.4% of the Earth's mass. This crust is made up oxygen, magnesium, aluminum, silicone, calcium, sodium, potassium and iron."

"Now jest a minute!" exclaimed Roddie. "An egg shell iss smooth an' dry, jest like Stanley Farquhar's head. He's so bald thet he gut ta put a chalk line on hiss forehead ta know where ta stop warshin' hiss face. But when I thinks a the Earth, I sees oceans, mountains, deserts, lakes an' prairies. Jest how thick iss this shell?"

"The continents are about 35 kilometres (21.7 miles) thick, while the floors of the oceans are about 7 kilometres (4.3 miles) thick."

"Yep simple," said John Alex, "In jest two days, tomorra will be yesterday, eh?"

"Go on," said Roddie.

"The Earth's mantle can be compared to the egg's albumen. It consists of oxygen, aluminum, silicon and iron and makes up 68.1% of the Earth's mass. The Earth's core, similar to the egg yoke, contains mainly nickel and iron and makes up about 31.5% of the Earth's mass. This core is an extremely hot, molten liquid, although it does have a small solid center about one kilometre in diameter."

"Yiss, yiss," said Roddie "Ass clear ass a crow in a bucket a milk, I knows all a thiss, so what?"

John Alex rolled his eyes and said, "Roddie, ya only knows 'bout ass much ass a pimple on a pig's arse, so zipper yer lips, eh?"

"Your 'so what' question is a good one, because its answer brings us closer to talking about weathering. But before we do, we should discuss the rock cycle. This is when rocks are formed, worn down and then reformed. It's not a short-term cycle and can take thousands or even millions of years.

"Rocks are divided into three main classifications depending upon how they were formed. Igneous rocks are formed under extreme heat and pressure and are finally brought to the surface by volcanoes, rock slides, or erosion. When exposed particles 'weathered' from these igneous rocks become cemented together, they form sedimentary rocks and through geologic time, this process has created large amounts of sedimentary rocks. The final rock type, metamorphic rocks are formed when either igneous or sedimentary rocks are changed by heat, moisture and pressure. And so here we stand, you Roddie holding a piece of granite which is igneous, John Alex has slate which is metamorphic, and I'm holding sandstone which is sedimentary."

Roddie nodded. "An' I suppose we're finally getting' ta weatherin'. Ask ya fer the time an ya gut ta start by tellin' me how ta build a clock."

John Alex tossed his stone at the oil can. It clanged and rolled again. He smirked and muttered, "Sometimes me talents even amaze meself!" He looked at me and winked. "Let's jump in yer truck and go in ta Jacob Mings an' have a coffee an' a doughnut… er three."

"Not 'till we hear 'bout hiss weatherin', said Roddie. "All ya thinks 'bout iss yer gut. Look at ya, double chins all the way down ta yer belt! Ya gut more chins than a Chinese phone book."

I suggested that we walk over to the woods to find some shade. It was getting hot standing there in the sun.

We made ourselves comfortable on stumps left by Johnny Cut An' Run that were amid some smaller hardwoods that for some unknown reason were left undamaged.

"Weathering is the first necessary step in the formation and on-going maintenance of soils and plants. It happens in three ways. Mechanical weathering is just what its name implies: the breaking apart of large rock into small pieces. This is done in a number of ways. Although not very common here in the Maritimes, rock slides on long, steep slopes can chip and break apart boulders as they smash and grind their way down the slope.

"However, a more common way is by freezing and thawing. These temperature changes stress the rock causing hairline cracks in the surface of the rock. Water seeps into these cracks, freezes and expands thus making the crack a bit deeper and larger. This allows more water to fill up the crack, and with more water comes increased expansion pressure as it turns to ice. Through this process a piece is eventually split from the rock.

"Rocks are also broken down mechanically by wave action, whether in a river or by the pounding waves at the beach. The fast moving water tumbles the stones knocking off tiny rough edges.

"And then there's wind. This process usually happens in desert areas where strong sand-laced winds actually sandblast and erode large rock faces."

Roddie leaned forward on his stump, elbows on knees and said, "Let me git thiss straight. Nature kin shoot liquid rocks outta a volcano. Thiss liquid contains minerals from outta deep in the Earth. The liquid cools an' hardens inta igneous rocks. Then Nature gut ta somehow grind these rocks down ta release the minerals. Right?"

"Yea, that's it in a nutshell. You with us on this John Alex?"

He grunted what I took to be a yes, then added that his guts were hollerin' for a doughnut…er three. They were. Sounded rather like my coffee maker.

"Ya said weatherin' happens in three ways," said Roddie.

"Yes, the second way is by a biological process where tree roots grow into rock crevices, expand as they grow, and force the rock apart.

"However, I find the third way, chemical weathering, to be the most fascinating process of the three. When was the last time that you boys were at the graveyard?"

John Alex, who usually blinks every other Wednesday, blinked. Roddie flicked his head like a rooster and said, "What in hell hass graveyards gut ta do with the number a teeth in China?"

"The headstones are a great example of chemical weathering."

"Yiss, yiss. Ya can't read the blurred inscriptions on those ole white ones."

"Them ones are marble, ya lunkhead," snorted John Alex.

Roddie gave him a stare that could nail a sign to a tree. He turned to me. "How long doess rocks last anaway?"

" I guess it depends upon the rock type and just where the rock is located. Rocks weather quicker in a warm, humid climate than they do where the climate is colder. However, in either location, marble for example, weathers twenty times faster than granite."

"Yiss, yiss, that's jest why I'm goin' ta hev a nice granite headstone when I puts on the wings an' white nightie."

John Alex just shook his head. "Yer so thin thet they'll prob'ly bury ya in a poster tube, an' don't be so sure ya'll even git ta peek inta the great behind, eh? I knows yer some alert fer signs a approachin' sin, but yer eyesight ain't thet good beins' thet ya wass around when Gabriel wass an apprentice trumpeter."

Roddie did crack a faint but fleeting smile. "So how doess the *marble* headstones weather? An' Jin Alek, why don't ya go an' find somethin' dangerous ta do?"

"Mainly by rain." I said. "Raindrops falling through the air absorb a small amount of carbon dioxide and thus become a very weak carbonic acid. Over a long period of time this weak acid slowly dissolves the marble. But, this process is speeded up in modern times because of acid deposition and acid rain. These days, airborne pollution often carries sulphur dioxide and nitrogen oxide. Unfortunately, when these gases combine with water they form much stronger sulphuric and nitric acids."

"Stanley Farquhar must a been standin' in thet acid rain, him bein' ass bald ass a peeled egg," observed Roddie.

"Let's go get a coffee an' a bunch a doughnuts. Youse guy's 'ill haff ta pay though, I'm so broke I can't buy oats fer a nightmare." And with that John Alex wheeled around and trundled over to my truck. He walked with his head down, much like a goose in a thunderstorm.

"Thet man should think 'bout cuttin' back on food," said Roddie. "He's gittin' a serious case of posterial exuberance."

"What in heaven's name is that?"

"A double measure a arse," chuckled Roddie.

Ming's Café hasn't changed much over the years. There's the counter with six vinyl-covered stools that children like to sit on and spin around, a row of booths down the right side and a scattering of tables around the rest of the dining area.

John Alex led us to a table in the corner. We sat and made small talk and soon I saw our waitress coming. Darn, today it just had to be Helen. Helen the Hun, who was well past her sell-by date, had recently been divorced from her third husband and by the way she was dressed she was trolling for unlucky number four.

She minced over to our table wearing a skirt the size of a fly swatter, and through her bee-stung lips, and a mouth so big that when she smiled she got lipstick on her ears, asked us in a husky voice, "Coffee, tea, er me boys?"

Roddie turned and looked her over. "Helen, how come yer not wearin' enough ta wad a shotgun with? Ya looks like ya were poured inta what few clothes yer wearin' an' forgot ta say when."

"It's the new me big boy, like it?"

"Yiss, yiss but yer bra size apparently iss larger than yer I.Q."

"Yea, I *am* rather fortunate there," she said as she took our orders and swayed back to the kitchen. She walked like her G string was out of tune.

John Alex, who hadn't blinked even once, remarked that she had been in so many motel rooms that she should change her name to 'Gideon'. Roddie informed us that she had so many facelifts that there was nothing left in her shoes.

As we sat drinking our coffee, Roddie put down his cup, wrung out his scraggly moustache, and said, "So far I gut the idea thet rocks gut ta be broken down, but yer last comment 'bout the acids gut me stumped. Seems ta me thet if ya gut too much acid floatin' 'round, yer kinda up thet famous creek."

"You're right. But let me finish describing how forest soils become more acidic and why. Nature relies on the chemical action of acids to help release the elements bound up within rocks. This allows these elements such as calcium, potassium, and phosphorous to be absorbed by plant and tree roots and be used for their growth. But don't forget, forest soils are usually, although not always acidic. The yearly accumulation of needles which drop off softwoods is a good example. When rain water percolates through this needle mat it leaches some carbon and becomes a mild carbonic acid."

"Hold yer harse! What doess ya mean *leaches*?"

I hesitated. Just then Helen the Hun was over by the counter making a fresh pot of coffee.

"Look at what Helen's doing behind you." Roddie twisted around and looked while John Alex sat there and didn't even blink. They both commented together that Helen was just making coffee.

"Think about how the process works. The crushed coffee beans are placed into the coffee maker and then water is poured in. The water percolates down through the coffee bean particles and the water soluble chemicals (the coffee) are picked up by the water and washed down into the coffee pot. But the insoluble crushed coffee remnants are left behind. This is an example of leaching. The same process happens when the rain water percolates down through the needle mat on the forest floor."

"I sees, so why iss thiss acid important?"

"Well, when this mild acid comes in contact with small stones or rocks it very, very slowly releases the elements bound within these rocks. In short, it weathers them."

"Now back ta yer comment, ya said thet we can hev too much acid floatin' around in Nature. Explain thet."

"Nature buffers and balances many forest soils by changing the crop that grows on these soils. While softwoods usually deposit acidic needles, the leaves of many hardwood species are less acidic or even slightly alkaline so that their leaching lessens the soils acidity."

"Jest like we puts lime on the fields, eh?" said John Alex.

"Yes. But now we have the problem of acid deposition and acid rain and, as I said before, these pollutants carry much stronger acids and have, are, and will, cause trouble. They've upset the delicate acidic balance in some lakes to the extent that aquatic life can't survive. To temporarily fix this problem, lime has been spread on the ice to lessen the acidity in ponds and lakes that have become barren of most aquatic life."

"Well," said John Alex, "the doughnuts are done so let's git back ta the pit an' git Roddie's truck so's I kin git home. Martha's makin' cheese an' ham biscuits an' I likes them with lasses an' tea."

During our drive back to the gravel pit, Roddie, who was squished in the middle of the truck seat, said, "Yer gettin' so big ya'll soon haff ta wipe yer butt with a rag on a stick! An' keep gettin' any fatter an' yer bathtub'll begin ta develop stretch marks! Must haff ta use a lotta soap!"

"Ya, I knows. Ya see, it's me condition, eh?"

"Yer condition?"

"Ya, I gut the dissmals."

"The what?" asked Roddie.

"I think he means that he's suffering from depression," I said.

"Yep, that's what I said. Since my brother died, I jist can't keep me spirits up, eh? They're up an' down jist like a politician's hand on 'lection day. But it's gettin' worse 'cause now my good feelins last jist 'bout ass long ass thet politician's promise. Seems ta help when I eats. So I eats."

"Wal, Jin Alek, why didn't ya tell me! I hed the black dogs lass year. Fer a coupla months I wass feelin' sadder than a country song. Jean made me go ta see ole Doc MacKinnon. He said thet I had a chemical imbalance in me brain an' gave me some little pills ta take. Three weeks later I wass feelin' on top a the world. Bin fellin' good effer since. Even doin' the horizontal hula agin."

"Ya means thet I kin git back ta feelin' good jist by takin' little pills?" He actually blinked. "An' I figgered thet I wass dyin'. Martha said thet I wass gettin' so sad thet I should be wearin' a shroud, eh?"

On that note I turned in to the gravel pit and parked the truck. As we walked across the pit Roddie asked, "Doess all a the plant elements come from rocks? Ya mentioned ones thet I'm familiar with in farmin' such as phosphorus, potassium, calcium, an' magnesium. What 'bout other elements?"

"Good question. Nitrogen, carbon and sulphur are obtained from the atmosphere, not rocks."

Roddie's green 1967 International was parked over at the edge of the pit near three partially moss-covered boulders.

"Before you boys go, there's one other thing I'd like you to think about. What do you see when you look at those boulders?" I asked.

"Rocks with moss on em?" ventured Roddie.

"Yes, but actually what you see is the initial, or a first formation, of soil. See those small white circular spots on the high points of the rock?"

"Yiss, yiss, 'pears ta be bird crap."

"Well, it's not, it's…"

"Roddie!" said John Alex, "I gut ta see Doc MacKinnon, so's I'll take yer truck an' you kin go home with him, eh?"

"Yiss, yiss go ahead, yer mind issn't here with us anaway. You wass sayin'?"

As John Alex drove out of the pit I said, "I was going to say that what's on the rock are lichens. You see them covering not only rocks, but also on soil. Have you noticed the tiny, perhaps ¼ inch tall, lichens with the red 'hats'?"

Roddie nodded. "Yiss, yiss we calls em British soldiers."

"Right. These lichens grow on soil, mossy logs, and decaying stumps. British soldiers help break down wood and recycle elements. There are also other well known lichens such as reindeer moss, and those you see hanging from branches. Those are called old man's beard."

"I offen wondered if'n these tree lichens were takin' anathin' from the tree."

"No, these lichens are just using the tree as a place to live, just the same as when you sit on a stump, you take nothing from the stump."

"So how doess they live?"

"Another good question. Let's look closely at this lichen on the boulder."

Roddie smiled, "Yer referrin' ta the bird crap?"

"Yes. These type of lichens are called crustose meaning "crusty." The two other types growing in other places are foliose (leafy) and fruticose (shrubby). But back to these crusty rock lichens. They're pretty neat because, first, they consist of a fungal part which soaks up water, and a second part, an alga, which can use sunlight to photosynthesise food. So a lichen consists of a fungus and alga. These work together getting their elements from sunlight, air, and water. During this process they give off a slight carbonic acid or other chemicals which weather the rock thus helping to create soil. Look closely, see that faint discolored ring surrounding the lichen?"

"Yiss, yiss, looks like a moat 'round a castle."

"That discoloration is in fact evidence of the acidic action. Over many, many years the lichen creates a thin bit of soil around it. After a long time, more complex leafy or shrubby lichens, or perhaps these mosses which we can see growing lower on this boulder will take over the process and replace the crusty lichen. So if we were to take a knife, and scrape even this initial crusty lichen off, we may be undoing centuries of Nature's patient work.

"And something else. It's been discovered that lichens are very sensitive to air pollution. They're now being used as bio-indicators to assess levels of industrial and urban air pollution. Unfortunately the increased pollution of the last 100 years is a serious threat to the health of lichens."

Roddie nodded. "Yiss, yiss, an' not only to lichens. My, my, us humans iss sure crappin' in our nest. But it's interestin' how givin' time, Nature kin even heal a scar like a gravel pit. Who would a thunk it."

Roddie then paused. "Ya know, Jin Alek iss my best friend an' I thinks thet I'm hiss. Why didn't he tell me thet he hed the black dogs? I could a helped him."

I smiled. "He didn't tell you, for the same reason that you didn't tell him. You both think that it's somehow a sign of weakness. And it's not that at all. It's a simple chemical imbalance that can be fixed."

"Humph! How comes ya knows so much 'bout it?"

"I have it too."

"Who would a thunk it."

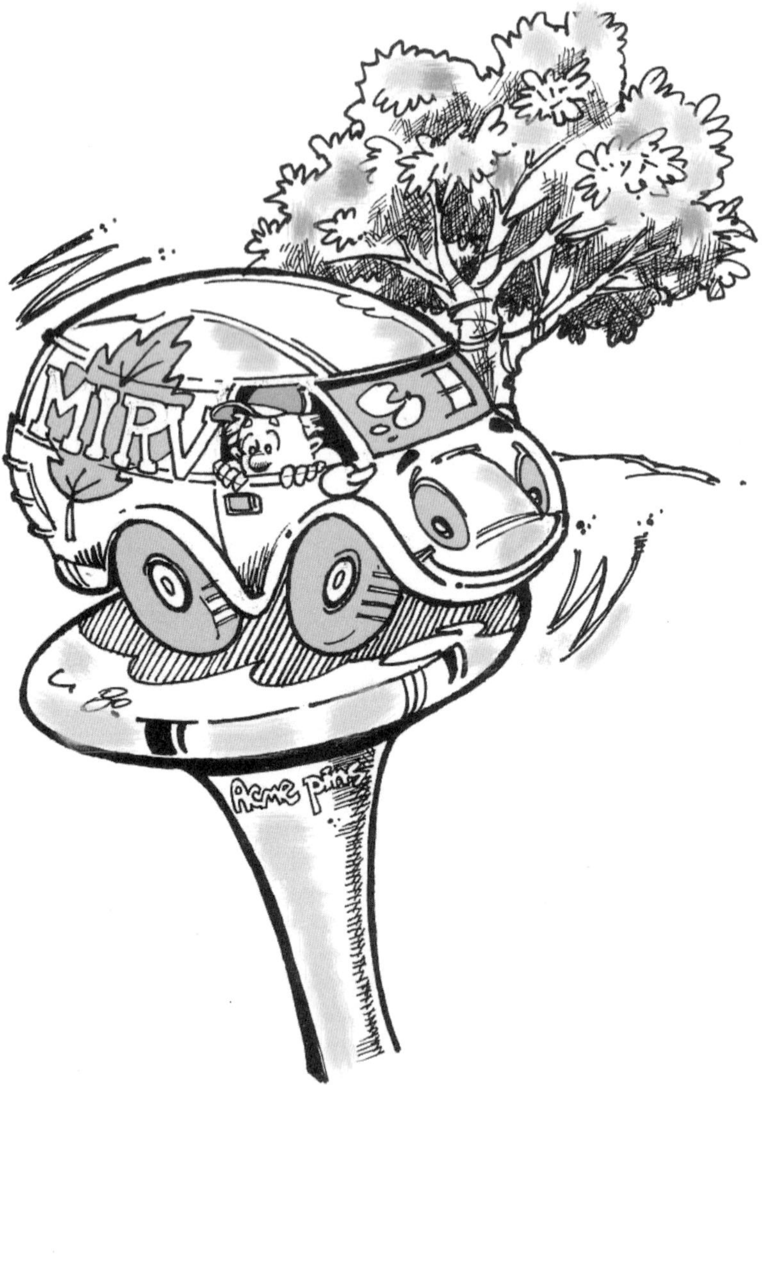
MIRV
Acme pins

THE SCHOOL VISIT

You can teach students a lesson for a day;
but if you can teach them to learn by creating curiosity,
they will continue the learning process
as long as they live.
- C.P. Bedford

"Uncommonly fine large day, what!"

I looked up from my desk and there stood Roddie. John Alex soon lumbered into my office.

"Morning boys, what brings you guys into Big Spoon Cove on such a beautiful morning."

"Me an' Jin Alek are jest passin' through. Headin' fer Northport ta pick up some parts fer hiss tractor."

I couldn't help but notice John Alex. He stood there and I'd describe him as 'beaming.' I remarked that he appeared to be quite pleased with the world.

"Yiss, yiss," said Roddie. "Since he gut hiss formaldehyde changed Jin Alek's bin steppin' 'round like a bean-fed harse. Ole Doc MacKinnon fixed him up with pills an' he ain't been the same since. Hev ya Jin Alek?"

"By gum thet stuff even makes yer sticker peck up, eh! Feelin' me ole self agin."

"Anahow, we gut ta be motorin'. What are ya up ta taday anaway?"

asked Roddie.

I told him that I was going over to the school at one o'clock to talk to the grade-three class about how a tree grows.

"Issn't thet Mrs. Major's class?"

"Yes, why do you ask?"

"Ya'll see," smiled Roddie.

As I walked over to the school, I wondered what Roddie meant. The Majors had moved to Big Spoon Cove last summer and she began teaching in September. Apart from our brief telephone conversation, I hadn't met her, but I guessed that that would soon change.

The school was starting to show its age. Built in 1894, the red bricks needed repointing, the once bright yellow trim needed a good scrape and repaint, and the heavy front door needed to be cleaned and revarnished. It looked shabby inside too.

As I walked down the hall I met Beverley MacKay, the grade-nine teacher. I asked her where Mrs. Major hung her hat.

She smiled and said, "Second floor, Room 22. Good Luck!"

Wonder what *she* meant I thought as I climbed the worn hardwood stairs.

I peeked into Room 22. There at her desk sat Mrs. Major.

She was a large, roomy woman who didn't seem so much as to be dressed, perhaps more like upholstered. She would certainly never ignite a clothing revolution. Her hair looked like my old orange tomcat when he got singed by a fire. And her face, it was wrinkled like a puddle in a hurricane.

She spotted me. "Come in. Who are you and what do you want?"

I approached, cap in hand, and stammered, "Ah, I'm...I'm here to talk to your class about how a tree grows Mrs. Major."

"Oh. Sit over there. We start in seven minutes. Sharp!"

I sat.

At two minutes to one the class entered as a group and took their

THE SCHOOL VISIT 35

seats. Mrs. Major, speaking in capital letters, bid them a good afternoon, introduced me and my topic, then marched to the back of the classroom. There she stood, back rigid and arms folded across her ample bosom thus shielding it from a surprise assault by any hormone-crazed third-grader.

"Good afternoon all," I said. "Mrs. Major told you that I'm going to talk to your about how a tree grows. Well, it's not going to happen quite that way."

At this, Mrs. 'Sergeant' Major gave me a look that would loosen bowels. I think she even showed her teeth, but perhaps it was just her upper denture dropping.

I walked over to a student wearing a tee shirt with BUM across the front. "I sat where you're sitting when I was here in grade three. I know I would've fallen asleep if someone stood up front for two hours and told me how a tree grows. What do you think?" I asked, looking around at the class.

Apart from Mrs. Major, most heads nodded.

"So I've decided to talk to you about magic. And it's magic that's all around us. Now, I've brought MIRV with me today. Know what that is? It's a Magic Imagination Roving Vehicle. You all have one. Even Ser...er, Mrs. Major," (although I thought this was surely straining even the strongest imagination).

"Here's how it works. Using our imaginations we can make ourselves, and MIRV any size we want, so let's imagine MIRV to be a little yellow school bus that's the size of a pinhead. When I say, 'Let's go', we'll all take a seat in our little bus and go on an imaginary tour inside that red maple tree at the front of the school. The big tree with the swing. Know the one I mean?"

There as a chorus of 'yays'. I had them.

"Ok. Now before we go, let's divide that tree into three sections. What can we call the part of the tree with leaves - where stuff is made?"

A little girl in a front seat said, "A factory?"

"Great, that's the factory. Now, what can we call the roots of the tree where stuff is taken in or stored?"

BUM guessed, "A warehouse?"

"Ok, so what connects these two together."

No response, so I suggested that we call the trunk of the tree the highway with other storage areas located along this road.

"Now, before we plan where we'll go first, there's something I want you all to think about. That tree with the swing is solid…right? If you ran into it it would hurt…right?

There were a chorus of yesses.

"Ok, now here's the magic. At one time, that tree was nothing but a bunch of carbon dioxide gas. Do you know what a gas is?" Most students nodded (and most students plus Mrs. Major looked at me like I didn't have elastic in both my socks). "So how can a gas, which is part of the air that we breath, turn into a tree?"

A little guy in the second row said that it must be magic, just like Christmas.

A hand shot up. "Who's goin' to drive MIRV? I want to!"

"No," I said, "I'd better drive 'cause you don't have your license yet."

Another hand. "Kin Mrs. Major come too?"

"Sure, she can sit in the back." This warranted another broadside of daggers my way. Perhaps the Sergeant thought she should drive, but it's my MIRV, so I'm afraid that she's S.O.L.

I turned and sketched a tree on the blackboard showing the crown, trunk, and roots. Next to the crown I printed *FACTORY*; beside the roots I drew a little sign saying *WAREHOUSE - SHIPPING AND RECEIVING*. I then drew a dotted line entering a tree root, passing up through the trunk which I had labelled *HIGHWAY* and exiting into the air from the factory. Above the drawing I sketched a big smiling sun.

"There. We'll start our journey down in the earth near the roots and follow the dotted line. Everyone ready?"

"Let's go!" They shouted.

"Ok class, we're now in the soil. It's dark so I'll turn on MIRV's lights. Notice that there are little puddles of water and little caves full of air through the soil. And there are many whitish roots around MIRV. These are the roots of a fungus that attached itself to our maple tree's roots.

"Whoa! See that? A soil beetle just scurried in front of us. I'll stop MIRV for a minute before we enter the fungus root. When you look outside MIRV you'll see all kinds of life. There's bacteria, tiny soil critters such as springtails, mites, little beetles, and over to our right is a big long centipede and even an earthworm! Notice that some of the little soil critters are munching on bacteria or fungus, while others are hunting and eating some of the little critters. Although when you walk on the soil you never see it, the soil is really full of life.

"Ok, let's enter the fungus, but I must drive carefully because it's a busy place."

In our imaginary trip through the fungus I told the class that we were being passed by little trains hauling wagons full of elements such as nitrogen, phosphorus, and also barrels full of water to feed the tree. I said that we were also meeting trains coming our way that were hauling sugar. This was produced at the tree's factory, sent down to the warehouse, then taken out and given to the fungus. The fungus used this sugar as its food.

"So you see class, the fungus helps the tree grow, and in return the tree helps the fungus grow."

"Like, a cornucopia of awesomeness," muttered BUM. Since I had told him that I had sat at his desk we were now long-time buddies.

"Hang on class, this may be bumpy because we're now going to enter the root."

As we journeyed within the crooked tree root, I explained that tree roots were something like a large system of shallow underground branches. That they had important jobs to do such as holding up the tree, anchoring it, binding the soil among the roots so that it wouldn't wash away, and searching the soil around the tree for water and elements.

A little girl at the back of the class asked, "Why are roots so crooked?"

"That happens when the sensitive growing root tips come up against hard objects such as rocks or other roots and have to steer around them."

"Ya, but, how come these root tips don't like, get hurt when they, like, bump inta stuff?" asked another little boy with flaming red hair. "I sure do!"

"That's another good question. Each root tip has a protective cap, I guess you could think of it as a little bicycle helmet, and roots also purposely "leak" substances that help lubricate the outside of the root and make it easier to burrow through the soil."

I went on to tell them that the roots also acted as a storage warehouse, especially in the winter. That trees in this part of the world prepare for winter by storing their food in the roots and that's why we called it *WAREHOUSE – SHIPPING AND RECEIVING*. This food or energy stays in the roots until the warming spring sun awakens the tree and the sap starts to "run" up the tree to supply the buds with food so the tree will leaf out and be able to make food in the "factory" for growth.

"This brings us to the question of transportation. In a tree this is done by pipelines, something similar to blood vessels that are used in our bodies to transport blood. But before we enter one of these pipelines in MIRV, let's talk about them.

"The pipelines are actually cells that connect with each other to form bundles of pipelines. I'm going to pass this around."

Last night I had dropped in to Ming's Café, got a handful of drinking straws and put an elastic band around them.

THE SCHOOL VISIT

"The bundle of straws that's being passed around represents how the pipelines, which as I said are connected cells, are arranged within the roots and trunk.

"One set of pipelines carries water and elements up from the roots, through the trunk and into the leaves. These pipes are called the xylem. The other connected cells, known as the phloem, are the pipes that carry sugars made by the leaves down to the roots. But there is one exception. During the spring, when the tree is awakening, the flow is reversed and instead, the phloem cells, or pipelines, carry elements which was previously stored for the winter, up to feed the emerging leaves. The phloem cells continue to do this until the leaves are large enough to produce sugar themselves."

Just then a bell rang announcing a ten-minute break for the class. They quickly filed out.

The Sergeant Major marched toward me in what I imagined was similar to a calvary charge minus the horse and bugle.

"What a bunch of twaddle! MIRV and pipes indeed! I never heard such rubbish! You must be more professional and scientific…but what can you expect from someone who only works in the woods!"

I had really tried to like her, but immediately stopped that futile experiment. I whirled around and printed $6\ CO_2 + 6\ H_2O = C_6H_{12}O_6 + 6\ O_2$ on the blackboard.

"You be the teacher Mrs. Major. Please explain this equation to me."

She stared at it vacantly.

"I don't teach chemistry," she snorted contemptuously.

"No? Well, when I'm finished today, your grade-three class will know what this means. I suggest that you pay attention and get over your 'my way or the highway' and your 'woods work' is uniquely suited to people with limited intelligence mentality!" I really wanted to tell her that she was like a barnacle on the arse of progress, but didn't. After all, that wouldn't be professional – perhaps only scientific.

She turned and left in a huff, which was probably a popular way for her to travel. I erased the 'chemistry' equation and sat at the desk and tried to calm myself.

After another five minutes the bell announced the beginning of the next class. I asked questions about what they learned during our first period. They were all answered, and I must add, answered with enthusiasm. Sergeant Major squeezed into a desk at the rear of the class and looked like a hen with a broken egg inside her.

"Ok. We're now in MIRV and will enter one of the pipelines in the roots. It'll eventually take us up the tree, out a limb, and end up in a leaf. But first, two questions. Which pipe should we go up in, and second, what will be carrying MIRV along?"

BUM, bless his little heart, said, "The "z" one, and it'll be full of water."

"Right, but even though it sounds like it begins with a 'z' it actually starts with an 'x'. I printed it on the blackboard, x-y-l-e-m. "And the xylem will be full of water and…?"

"Elements" said a girl sitting next to BUM.

"Right again. So it's a good job that MIRV's waterproof with all this element-filled water rushing past us."

As we began our imaginary journey through the root's xylem and toward the tree's trunk

I explained to the class how our tree actually grew in height and diameter. That the outside of the tree was protected by a "skin" called bark. That the bark covered the phloem or inner bark. That in the phloem, cells formed the pipes taking sugars made in the leaf factory down to the roots, and while doing so, dropped off nutrients to feed the adjacent layers of cells called the cambium.

"So we have the outside bark of the tree, the inner bark or phloem, then the cambium. The cambium is where the tree actually grows. Here's how it does it. During the time of year when plants are growing, the cells in the tree's cambium keep growing by dividing, so that each growing season a new layer or "ring" is added to the thickness of the tree. While the tree is getting fatter, it's also getting taller because the cambial cells at the end of twigs are also dividing thus making the twig longer.

"And this brings up two other new words; "cellulose" and "lignin." What happens is that the sugar molecules manufactured in the leaf factory are attached to the walls of the tiny growing cambial cells. In other words, the sugars from the leaves form cellulose and lignin – and this combination of cellulose and lignin makes up what we call 'wood' and, as you all know, a tree is made of wood."

I told the class that the water had now carried us up the tree, out a large limb to a small twig and that we were now about to enter a leaf.

Mrs. Major spoke out in capital letters. "How did the water get up the tree? Was it pumped by the roots?"

Contrary to what I thought, she was actually listening.

"Good question. Let's just hold that question for a few minutes though, until we explore the leaf.

"We'll stop MIRV here just within the leaf. If you look up through the glass roof of our little bus you can see the top of the leaf. Notice that the cells are transparent so they'll allow sunlight to come in."

"Just like the skylight in my bedroom," said BUM. "Mine leaks. Does the leaf's roof leak?"

"No, it doesn't my friend," I replied. "And just below the roof of the leaf is a layer containing many cells. These cells appear green in colour because each cell contains what are known as chloroplasts. They give the leaf its green colour, but more importantly, this is where the magic happens. These little chloroplasts take air, water, and elements from the soil, light from the sun, and magically turn it into wood. Think about it. It's one of the important miracles of Nature. It's called photosynthesis.

"Just like Santa," sighed a little girl in the front row.

"An' the Easter Bunny," whispered her friend.

"Now class, there's another layer of cells under the magic layer of chloroplasts, but there're kind of spongy and loose. They're that way so that air and water can easily move through them. You'll understand why when we look at the bottom 'skin' of the leaf. The underside of a leaf is where two other important processes take place. One is breathing, the other is getting rid of excess water."

"I get rid of excess water by peein' in the toilet," proudly announced BUM.

"I hadn't thought of trees peeing,"class laughed. Mrs. Major scribbled vigorously on her note pad. "It's more like breathing. You guys can see your breath as a white little cloud on a cold winter's day. Right?"

Everyone nodded (even Mrs. Major).

"The little cloud that you see is made up of moist air condensing into tiny water droplets as they come in contact with the cold air. Trees breathe tiny water droplets too. The leaf only uses one or two percent of the water which came up from the roots for photosynthesis, the rest is removed from the leaves through tiny pores in the bottom of the leaf. These are called stomates and they're something like our lips because they have cells called guard cells on each "lip" that can open or close the stomate. This allows the leaf to control the elimination of water and the intake and expulsion of gas. We know that air contains carbon dioxide. The air enters the little mouths, or stomates, and the carbon dioxide is used by the leaf in the photosynthesis process. Remember class, photosynthesis

THE SCHOOL VISIT 43

is simply carbon dioxide, water and sunlight changing into plant sugars and oxygen. The sugars are used by the plant for growth and development and the oxygen is passed out of the leaf through the stomates. Pretty neat isn't it?"

There was a chorus of 'cools'.

"How much water comes out of a tree in a day?" asked the little guy with the red hair.

"Well, it depends, but a full-grown tree can give off about 1200 to 1400 litres each day during the growing season," I answered. "And that's just one tree. Think what forests are giving us in water and oxygen each day."

"Awesome," mumbled BUM.

"How much oxygen?" asked Mrs. Major.

"I can't give you the exact amount, but I think that one average size mature tree gives off enough oxygen to keep eight or ten people breathing for a day. I'll check this out and get back to you.

"A little while ago, your teacher asked how the water gets from the roots up to the very top of a tree. Now class, I happen to know that Mrs. Major does know, but asked this question so that I wouldn't forget to explain the process to you." (I was lying through my teeth, but I was trying to be 'professional'). Mrs. Major smiled her thanks.

"This is also a neat, or, as you say, cool process. But first, there are two more parts of the tree that must be explained to you."

I went to the blackboard again and drew a large circle. I drew an arrow pointing at the outside of the circle and printed *BARK*. Next, I drew a circle just a bit smaller within the bark circle and labelled it *PHLOEM*. Then another circle slightly smaller which I called *CAMBIUM*. I then drew a smaller circle leaving a larger space between it and the cambium circle and labelled it *SAPWOOD*.

"Now class, another name for the sapwood is one that you're already familiar with and it's xylem. Remember that bundle of drinking straws that I passed around?"

The students nodded.

"Well that's what the sapwood looks like."

I then drew a smaller circle near the center of my large circle and labelled it *HEARTWOOD*.

I turned and said, "The heartwood is actually old sapwood that's found in the center of the tree trunk. The heartwood no longer carries water up the tree and is usually darker in colour than the sapwood. It's darker because the heartwood is the tree's 'dump' or disposal area where the tree deposits excess gums, resins and other substances no longer necessary for its growth.

"So now that you know that, we'll find out how water is able to climb up through the straw-like tubes in the sapwood/xylem.

"Remember the sun that I drew above the sketch of the trees that I drew before?"

They nodded again.

"Well, today you learned that the sun is the energy source that powers the leaf's magical production of sugars from carbon dioxide and water. But the sun also does something else. The heat from the sun actually pulls the water up the tree. Here's how it works. When water is in a very small tube the water molecules tend to stick together. As water droplets are evaporated from the stomates, or little mouths found on the underside of leaves, the fact that the water molecules in the tiny tubes are bound together, pulls the tiny column of water up the tree to replace those water droplets that were removed from the leaf due to evaporation. It's the same as you sucking a milkshake up through a straw.

"Any questions?"

I answered questions on why the school's maple tree's leaves turn red in the autumn, how maple syrup is made, and why maple seeds have 'wings'.

"Well class, my time's nearly up, so I'll finish by saying that a tree is indeed magical. When you look at one, you now know that it's made from air, water and sunlight. And that although you can't see it, it's also a standing column of water. And oh, by the way, we left MIRV parked up inside a tree branch. But only you guys, Mrs. Major, and I know. We'll keep this our secret."

"Let's call our school tree, 'MIRV'!" hollered BUM.

Then the bell rang, and class was over.

As I erased the blackboard I could hear Mrs. Major approaching in her sturdy World War II type shoes.

"Thank you for coming today. I learned two lessons from you. How a tree grows and…ah…that I…"

"I understand Mrs. Major. It's been, like, a cornucopia of awesomeness."

We both laughed and I left promising to return some day. As I walked out past the big red maple with the swing I nodded, and silently thanked MIRV for its help.

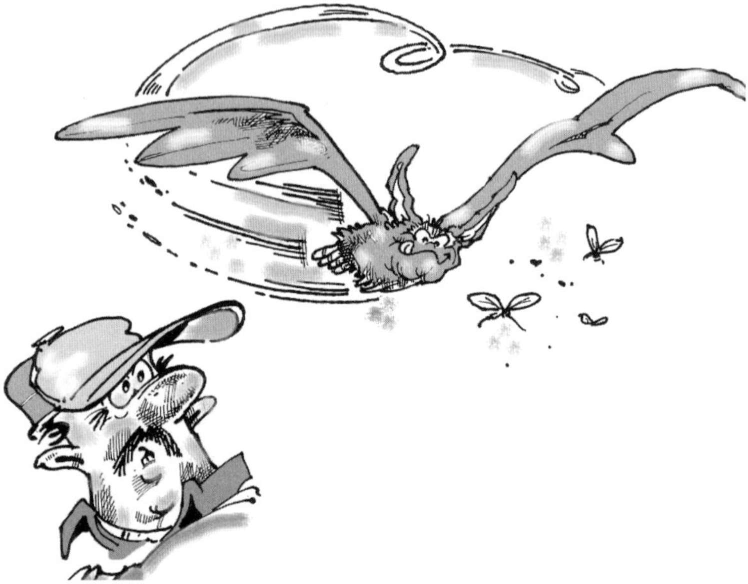

BARBERS, BLUES, BATS AND RATS

In all of Nature, diversity disguises underlying simplicity.
- John Maddox

Ed's Barber Shop is located next to the public wharf on Big Spoon Cove's main (and only) street. It's been there as long as I can remember. As was its owner Ed Reid. He's a short, rotund man who sports a permanent smile that peeks out from under a white moustache which contains enough hair to stuff a pillow.

Ed's shop takes you back to the 1950s. It's fitted out with an ornate but uncomfortable barber chair, five wooden Bass River chairs, a black cast-iron wood stove, and bottles of colourful hair tonics, bay rums, and of course, an assortment of shaving mugs, brushes, scissors, and hand-operated hair clippers.

Ed's is a relaxing place. And every haircut is an adventure.

At noon, on the last day of May, I walked over to Ed's to get a haircut. Since it was the end of the week and also pension-cheque time, the shop was full, so I stood leaning against the back wall to wait my turn.

Ed, who was just finishing deftly shaving around the village priest's rather large ears said, "Father, would ya like me ta mow er at least prune yer nose an' ear hairs? Bet ya could plant a peck a spuds in thet mess a hairy vegetation."

Father Brennan chuckled. "Perhaps you should Ed. I've been thinking that I'm getting deaf. Maybe it's only my, 'mess a hairy vegetation'. Speaking of which, are you able to smell anything through that luxurious rain forest under your own nose?"

"Ya gut me there Father," laughed Ed. He finished up and the priest got up to leave.

Old Harvey MacInnis, Roddie's uncle wobbled over and plopped in the barber chair. Poor Harvey's hands were so shaky that I bet he could thread a sewing machine when it was going. Ed threw the cape around him and asked, "Harvey, did ya hear that Annie Watson lost her husband Dave?"

"Yiss, yiss, damn careless a her. An her sech a pretty woman. Always minded me of a hen thet would lay nice brown eggs."

The door swung open and Tit Nipper marched in with the air of someone who had achieved something remarkable. Tit Nipper, whose right name was Jimmy Morrison, was at least four-foot eleven. He definitely displayed delusions of adequacy, but I once heard Roddie say that Tit Nipper was much too short to have high esteem.

I had taken Harvey's chair so Tit Nipper stood by the stove, arms crossed across his little chest and tried on a number of smiles until he found the one he liked. He then announced, "I gut bats in me shed, how kin I kill 'em?"

From the barber chair Harvey cackled, "I thought thet they wass all in yer belfry."

"I don't have a belfry. Ain't tall enough I guess. So, how does I kill the little buggers."

"Bats are beneficial to humans, why on earth do you want to kill them?" I asked.

Tit Nipper rose to a heady elevation of five feet on his toes. "Beneficial! Are ya crazy? The dirty little buggers go fer yer throat ta suck yer blood, er swoop down an' get tangled in yer hair. Beneficial me arse. Thought thet at least *you* would know thiss stuff!"

"I do know about bats, Tit. And they *are* beneficial."

"Well you an' yer book learnin's wrong. So there."

Tit Nipper's mind was made up. I knew that I'd be wasting my breath to try to convince him otherwise. I just shook my head and said nothing.

Tom MacKinnon was sitting next to me. He said, "I've always bin interested in bats. Tell *me* 'bout 'em."

"I guess bats are like anything else in Nature. People are afraid of snakes, bats, leeches – you name it. But when they learn about their lives and the necessary and important roles that these creatures play, they eventually get an appreciation for them.

"Bats are unique. They're the only mammal that can really fly – 'flying' squirrels just glide. The beneficial part to us is that bats can eat about half their own body weight in mosquitoes, moths, wasps, beetles and flies each evening. It's been discovered that bats eat 600 or more mosquitoes every hour that they're feeding.

"Now being mammals, the young are born alive and drink their mother's milk. The mother normally has one baby which is born around June or early July. It's difficult to observe, but for the first two weeks the baby bat clings to its mother, even when she's out flitting about catching insects at dusk or in the dark. The young bat can catch its own food when it's about a month old.

"Another neat thing is how bats actually catch insects. They do it by echo location. I'm told that the bats send out a high-frequency sound. When this sound hits an object or insect, the sound bounces back to the bat. It then knows where the object or insect is. If it's an object, the bat avoids it. But if it's a flying insect, the bat swoops in, grabs the insect with its wings and flips it into a pouch that's formed by the wing and tail membranes. The bat then simply eats the insect."

"Ya but...no but," said a rather agitated Tit Nipper. "I've seen 'em. They dive fer yer hair!"

"No they don't. They do dive and swoop around us, but that's where the mosquitoes are, and the bats are feeding on them; not trying to get themselves tangled up in our hair. Bats aren't stupid."

Tom asked how long bats can live, and where they actually do live.

"Ya, and when yer done tryin' ta answer thet question I gut one fer ya. How kin bats be beneficial when I sees 'em on TV suckin' the jessless blood outta a poor cow. Answer thet!"

"Well Tom, the little brown bat, which is the bat species found around here, can live for 20 or even 30 years. They like to live near wetlands because of the abundance of insects that are found there.

"As far as where they nest, it can vary from natural areas such a cavities on large trees, in caves, to house attics, barns, or even Tit Nipper's shed. They like warm, dark places located within about a quarter mile from a wetland."

"Ya, they're in me shed alright," chimed in Tit Nipper. "Come ta think 'bout it they weren't after me hair, but were lookin' ta suck blood from me neck."

"No they weren't. There are about a thousand species of bats around the world. And yes, some are vampire bats, but as I said before, our bat is the little brown bat and it's an insectivore which means that it eats insects. Vampire bats, the ones that live on blood, are found in tropical regions. And by the way, they don't "suck" blood. They puncture the skin and secrete a blood thinner with their saliva which causes the animal or human blood to run freely. They then simple lick the flowing blood."

Tom nodded and went over and took his place in the barber chair. Unfortunately, Tit Nipper sat in Tom's chair next to me.

"So, gettin' back ta me question, how doess I kill the bats in me shed?"

"Well Tit, I'm trying to show you that it's good to have bats on your property. It's quite clear that I've failed to do that. But for

Pete's sake don't kill them! Go out at dusk and find out where they're coming out of your shed. Then wait until they're all out and block their exit. You'll probably need a ladder."

Ed, who was apparently listening to our conversation snorted. "Yip, ya better have a ladder see'n that ya haff ta stand on a rock ta kick a duck in the arse."

Tit Nipper laughed. But not to be outdone, he replied, "Speakin' a arses, at least mine don't look like the two igloos thet you haul 'round behind ya."

And so it went that day at the barber shop. Comments like these would probably lead to shoot outs or at least fist fights in other places. What people from "away" find difficult to understand is that in Big Spoon Cove it's a form of comradery that probably began during earlier times. Times when life could be quickly lost at sea, in the coal mines, or in the woods. Rather than appear afraid the men resorted to humour. They discovered that a well-timed cutting retort could lighten the daily drudgery of hard physical and often dangerous work.

Shortly after moving to Big Spoon Cove 20 or so years ago, I met Roddie. I was soon verbally assaulted by his sharp comments. Confused, I had asked him why the insults and was told that people take themselves and their importance much too seriously. But, he had said with a wink, "Ya neffer, effer tease anaone ya don't like."

For some reason, I was in a pensive mood after I left Ed's Barber Shop. It was a bright sunny day, filled with a gentle salt-laced breeze. I walked to the end of the village wharf and looked out over the glittering waters of the cove.

For the first time, I realized that things had slowly but significantly changed during my 20 years of living in Big Spoon Cove. When I moved here there were about twenty cape-island fishing boats tied up here at the wharf. Now there were four. Then there was one pleasure boat; now six gently rocked against the wharf while three large sail boats swung at anchor in the cove.

Twenty years ago everyone did all their shopping in the village. Now the fish market, butcher shop, hardware store, garage, sawmill and grocery store were gone - as was the post office. Now people picked up their mail at an ugly nest of Canada Post mail boxes; gassed and coffeed up at the gas bar/convenience store; drove to the big box stores in New Harbour or Northport to do their shopping, and many also drove there to work.

Big Spoon Cove was indeed changing; from a vibrant, self sustaining village where Monday-morning washings fluttered in the breeze; to a bedroom community – where styrofoam coffee cups littered the ditches as people sped away to work.

I turned and slowly walked back to the office. It was sad, not only to see a way of life dying, but also a culture. People tell me that it's progress, tell me to 'get with it'. When asked, they define progress as 'growth' If that's the case, I guess that the tumour which I see infecting small business, fishing, farming, and a simpler lifestyle is indeed making progress.

Roddie was waiting at the office when I got back. "Uncommonly fine large day, what!" he said. "Took ya long 'nuff. Bin waitin' here fer haff an hour. Wants ta ask ya somethin'."

Roddie hesitated and stared at me. "What's wrong with ya? Ya looks like ya lost yer bess friend."

I told Roddie about my depressing thoughts of the disappearing traditional village way of life and the significant changes in how many people now live. I said that it seems that the ship is sinking and there's no lifeboat.

"Yiss, yiss, me an' the current first wife an' former sweetheart has had the same feelin's. Jean sez thet we're enterin' a society where individual values an' beliefs are different then ours. She sez thet people have bin frightened by how quick things change an' are gettin' more complicated. An' she's right when ya thinks 'bout it. Their grandfather had a farm; their father had a garden; an' now they hass a can opener. An' they thinks thet's progress.

"Yiss, yiss I sez to her, I kin fix me ole '67 International meself, but I read so much 'bout how ta take care of thet complicated armored personnel carrier thet ya calls a van thet I had ta give up readin'."

"Yes," I nodded, "and people are under more stress. Granted some of the stress is self imposed because of this instant-gratification craze that plummets people into substantial debt."

"Yiss, yiss. There's so many husbands an' wives workin' now thet it's the norm. Jean sez thet people gut to figger out the difference 'tween wants an' needs. Sez thet people are buyin' so much thet their houses are gettin' so heavy that they're sinkin' inta the ground an' thet it seems thet society iss goin' ta hell in a shoppin' cart.

"Course ass ya knows, most a yer money goess ta the government anaway so thet they kin either foolishly spend it in other countries ta make themselves look good, or ta line their own an' friends pockets 'stead a spendin' *our* money on things thet *we* need sech ass hospitals an' education an' the environment. I used ta kind a respect politicians but now I finds thet most a them cackles a lot but I ain't seen no eggs yet."

Are there no honest politicans Roddie?"

"I heard thet there wass one over in New Harbour, but it's prob'ly jest a rumor."

We went on to talk about relentless advertising that causes many people to see themselves as too fat, too wrinkly, too smelly, or driving the wrong vehicle. We discussed senseless wars, spreading violence, rising crime rates, drugs, environmental concerns, road rage, and even sound and light pollution.

"What do we do about it Roddie?"

"Wal, the way thet Jean and me sees it iss thet most a these things is outta our control, so we jist gut ta keep tryin' ta do the best we kin ta make a happy life fer ourselves. What we finds thet helps iss ta know an' do what makes ya feel good. With us it's the solitude an' stillness a the woods an' the camp."

By this time, I don't know why, but I felt better. "Before we took this verbal voyage through society's problems you said that you had a question."

"Yiss, yiss." Roddie hesitated. "I fergits…oh yiss! Jin Alek an' me wass talkin' 'bout what ya said 'bout recyclin' water the other day at the camp. An' he said thet ya said thet air iss recycled too. We can't figger out how thet could happen. Kin ya run thet by me? An' don't go tellin' me 'bout breathin' Churchill an' the boys air like ya did 'bout drinkin' their pee! Don't take a drink a water now but what I thinks 'bout it."

"Don't let the water thing bother you, but for your information you've now got atoms from snakes and birds and animals and long-dead humans in your lungs as we speak."

"I don't wanna hear 'bout it! Jist stick ta the air so's I kin explain it ta Jin Alek."

"Ok," I laughed. "Oxygen is found in three main areas; the atmosphere, hydrosphere, and lithosphere. In other words in the air, in the liquid part of the Earth, and in the Earth's crust and upper-most mantle."

"What does ya mean the Earth's crust? There's oxygen down there?"

"There sure is, just a minute." I rummaged through papers heaped in my 'file or recycle' cardboard box. "Here it is, a chart showing percentages of oxygen by volume. In the Earth's crust – 94.4%, in the hydrosphere – 33.00%, and in the atmosphere – 21.00%.[1]"

"Yiss, yiss, who would a thunk it. Where iss thiss oxygen at in the crust anaway?"

"It's found as part of the chemical make up of minerals, so it's a solid and not a gas. Now as I told you before, the Earth's crust is about 22 miles thick under the continents and about 4 miles thick under the oceans. So this is what we're referring to when we talk about the 94% oxygen found in the mineral composition of rocks. Don't confuse this with the oxygen which is found in topsoil as a gas and is so necessary for plant and soil organism's survival.

"The main source of new oxygen on land is made by plant photosynthesis. This uses the energy from the sun to combine carbon dioxide from the air with water to create sugars and oxygen. Oceans also produce oxygen. In fact, about 45% of new oxygen is created by ocean organisms called phytoplankton. However, there's also a third source for new oxygen. It's created by a process called photolysis where ultraviolet radiation breaks down water and nitrites in the atmosphere into free hydrogen and nitrogen atoms thus releasing oxygen."

"Yiss, yiss, so where does all thiss oxygen go?"

"Well, oxygen is consumed by respiration and decay mechanisms. As you know, trees 'breathe' in air, use the carbon dioxide, and emit oxygen. Humans, animals, and even bacteria breathe in air, consume the oxygen and breathe out the carbon dioxide. Oxygen is also lost through the chemical weathering of rocks."

"Stop the bus! Ya just gut through tellin' me thet there wass lots a oxygen in minerals. Now yer sayin' thet it's lost?"

"Didn't take you long to see that. The answer is yes and no. When organisms weather rocks they can release oxygen, as can plants and soil organisms when they extract minerals from rocks. However, chemical weathering does consume oxygen. A good example is the rust on your 1967 International truck. Rust happens when water comes in contact with iron. The water combines with the carbon dioxide in the air and becomes a weak carbonic acid. This acid slowly begins to dissolve the iron, and in doing so, some of it breaks down into hydrogen and oxygen. The oxygen then bonds with the iron as iron oxide – and that's what we call rust.

"In Nature, there's a red ferric oxide mineral called hematite which gives the red colour to many soils. To explain how oxygen in the air combines with the iron in the rock, I'll have to use the chemical symbols and write an equation."

I reached for a pad and wrote:

$$4\,FEO + 3\,O_2 \rightarrow 2\,FE_2O_3$$

Roddie stared at it and said, "Ya better 'splain it ta me. It's bin years since I worked out me lass equation in thermodynamics."

"It means that four molecules of iron oxide plus 3 molecules of oxygen creates two molecules of ferric oxide, also called hematite. From the equation you can see that molecules of air-borne oxygen are now bound to the iron.

"In oceans, oxygen is also bound up in sea shells. These are made of calcium carbonate ($C_A\,CO_3$) which is high in oxygen. As these shelled organisms die they are slowly covered on the ocean floor and eventually create limestone.

"Now, feel ready to explain this to John Alex?"

Roddie hesitated. "No, I don't thinks thet I'll bother. He's gut an I.Q. 'bout the same ass a pigeon. Doubt if'n he could even count ta twenty-one without pullin' hiss zipper down. But ya might ass well spoil me day. What did ya mean 'bout me havin' molecules from snakes an' birds, an' dead people in me?"

"Ah, no, poor old Churchill's urine bothered you, let's pass on that."

"Come on ya gommice, let me haff it."

I laughed. "Ok. Remember when we said that whatever is found on Earth or in the atmospheric envelope surrounding the Earth is held here by gravity? And that in effect the Earth has got to be a self-contained recycling spaceship?"

"Yiss, yiss, an' you jest explained ta me how oxygen iss produced but I don't think thet we recycle oxygen with snakes an' dead people so what are ya saying?"

---

[1] Regents Prep Earth Science. Retrieved January 16, 2007 from the World Wide Web: http://regentsprep.org/regents/earthsci/units/introduction/lithosphere.cfm

"It's not oxygen that I'm going to talk about. Air is made up of about 78% nitrogen, 21% oxygen, and the rest is argon and carbon dioxide. Argon is an inert gas which means that it enters our body with each breath we take, but, being inert, it isn't absorbed by our lungs. Now, since we only normally expel about 10% of the air in our lungs with each exhale, this means that atoms of argon actually remain within us for a short time. As they do in trees, rats, snakes, and indeed anything that breathes air, or was once living and breathed air. Each has exhaled their argon atoms back into the atmosphere to be recycled into other lungs. Don't forget, we all share the same air and this air is moved around the Earth by wind."

Roddie stared at me. "Wal, wal, it ain't enough thet I might consume a molecule er two a Churchill's pee in me water, now ya gut me inhalin' atoms thet were once in a sewer rat's lungs!"

"Yep, and that sewer rat might have been around during the days of the Black Death in England."

"Sorry thet I asked. But wait 'till I see's Jin Alek. I'll tell him thet he's gut some a hiss sister-in-law's atoms in him. That'll make him blink! Gut ta go."

I could hear Roddie chuckling to himself as he left my office. No doubt in search of his friend.

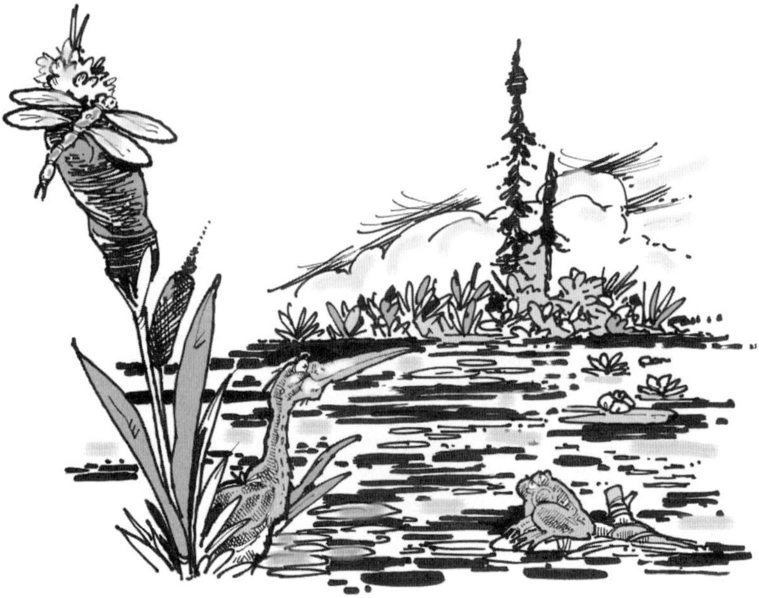

PONDS, BOGS AND OTHER THINGS WET

*One learns to hope that Nature possesses an
order that one may aspire to comprehend.*
- Chen Ning Yang
(1961 Nobel Physics Prize)

On Sunday night I had a phone call from Roddie. "Kin ya an' Frugal come out ta me new woodlot sometime this week? Grade-eight students hass some kinda Nature studies course an' wants ta talk ta me 'bout the pond on me woodlot next week. Ya gut ta kinna brush me up on thiss stuff 'fore they comes."

I told Roddie that I'd check with Frugal on Monday, but that I couldn't go until Friday. He said that Friday would be fine and promptly hung up.

Friday morning I picked up Frugal at the office and we drove out to Roddie's camp to get him. When we got there, Roddie had a hamper of sandwiches and a huge thermos, of what I supposed was tea, on the floor near the door. He was sitting at the table sharpening his pocket knife.

He looked at us with a twinkle in his eye and said, "Uncommonly fine large day, what! Give me yer knives an' I'll show ya how ta put a proper edge on em."

We did as we were told and Roddie went on to tell us that, although he used an oilstone for sharpening his knife, he didn't use oil.

"Nope, oil jest clogs up yer stone, I uses vinegar instead. Don't believe in shavin' with me knife, *I'm* inta splitin' hairs, *then* yer knife iss sharp!"

As he deftly honed our pocket knives I poured us all a cup of tea.

"Roddie," I said, "before we go out among the blackflies and mosquitoes, why don't we talk about ponds here; then we'll go out."

"Jist what I wass thinkin' meself. Where doess we start?"

"Let's first look at ponds in general," said Frugal, "and talk about how ponds and lakes function. Then look at the successional development of ponds and the organisms and plants that normally live there."

"Can't argue with thet," said Roddie.

Frugal nodded for me to begin.

"There are four zones within a pond. Beginning at the edge of the pond there's the emergent plant zone, then the floating-leaf zone, next is the submersed plant zone, and finally the deepest part of the pond where there are no rooted plants. This results in the usual plant locations in the pond. So a typical pond would have grasses, sedges and cattails growing in the shallow waters surrounding the pond. These underwater plant stems provide habitat and protection for frogs, algae, insects, snails and small fishes.

"In the floating-leaf zone you'll find the large flat-leaved lilies, water ferns and duckweed. Because water lilies shade the bottom from sunlight, bottom-growing plants aren't usually found here, but on the underside of these leaves you'll often find algae and also snail and perhaps mayfly eggs.

"The submersed plant zone is interesting because here we find pond weeds and other water weeds. These are actually flowering plants that grow completely submerged. However, their flowers will be pollinated above the water, the seeds will develop, sink to the bottom of the pond, germinate, and grow under water."

"Yiss, yiss, makes it easier ta understand when ya breaks it down inta zones. Ass ya were talkin' I wass thinkin' a me pond, an' what ya jest said iss what it looks like."

"Before we go to your woodlot, I'd like to point out how these plants actually energize your pond Roddie," said Frugal. "You see, energy from the sun allows the plants to photosynthesise and manufacture energy in their green leaves. The leaves are eaten by plant eaters such as some types of beetles, algae, water fleas, mayfly nymphs, and crustaceans. These plant eaters in turn are the food for carnivores such as beetle larvae, dragonfly nymphs, and small fish. Next these small carnivores are fed on by larger fish, which are also carnivores. And finally, perhaps an osprey will plunge into the water and grab a larger fish for its meal; or you may catch one and make it your meal."

"Quite a chain a who eats who," said Roddie. "What happens ta the ones who gits ta live?"

"They eventually die and decompose. Since nothing is wasted in Nature, their energy is now available to the green plants," said Frugal.

"Somethin' like manure I guesses. Let's go ta the woods. Jin Alex should be there by now, he hed ta renew his subscription fer some little feel-good pills first thing thiss mornin'."

As we slowly drove down Roddie's camp road to the main highway Roddie suddenly said, "Speakin' a pills somehow minds me a somethin' Jean said the other day. She was tellin' me thet a queen bee mates once an' then kin lay fertile eggs fer five er so years. When ya thinks 'bout it this iss amazin'. Doess ya know how thiss works?"

I was driving and admitted that I certainly didn't know.

Frugal said, "That's an interesting question, as are most questions about insects. The young queen bee flies out two or three times and mates with a drone bee. Near her ovaries is a little sac that the sperm is collected in. Attached to this sac is a gland that actually produces food for the sperm and these nutrients keep the sperm alive. I read somewhere that the sperm can be kept alive for up to eight years! So when the queen lays each egg from her ovaries, she also releases a single sperm to fertilize that egg as it passes from her body."

"Yiss, yiss, the more ya learns the curiouser an' curiouser ya gits. Amazin'!"

I turned off the highway and entered the rough road into Roddie's old gravel pit. John Alex was standing beside his Chevy truck grinning.

"Did ya think ta take a lunch Roddie?"

"Yiss, yiss, least ya could a said hello first. Yer gettin' so fat thet ya must hev 'bout two acres a denim in the arse a yer pants. Yer gettin' outta shape."

John Alex laughed. "Round iss a shape. But at least I ain't like you, eh? We could boil ya fer a week an' still not get a decent stew, ya gut about ass much meat on ya ass a robin's instep, eh?"

We laughed and chatted as we walked along the narrow trail that let to the pond. When we got there we stood swatting blackflies and looked at the pond.

"Ya mentioned duckweed," said Roddie. "What doess it look like?"

"I don't see any here now, but later in the summer you'll probably see it. It's a tiny floating herb and actually one of the smallest of the seed plants. However, it doesn't often produce seeds, it usually reproduces by cell division. This allow it to form dense green mats on quiet waters. If you pick up one of the tiny plants you'll see a little short, straight root which hangs below the plant. As the name implies, duckweed is a favourite food of waterfowl."

We made our way around the pond. Frogs shrieked and plopped into the water. Frugal suddenly stopped.

"Look, isn't that a beaut?"

There, on a large flat rock, sat a painted turtle.

"It's just an old turtle, eh? Iss there somethin' special 'bout 'em?"

"Yiss, yiss, Jin Alek there iss. They frequently moves faster then yerself."

John Alex grunted. Frugal smiled and said, "I haven't seen too many painted turtles around this area. They're more common in other parts of the province. Turtles are interesting for a number of reasons. For example, they're air breathers like ourselves, but they can do something that we certainly can't. They can lie buried in the mud at the bottom of a marsh, pond, lake, or slow moving river for months; and never once come up for air.

"Another reason is their reproduction. Female turtles dig a shallow pit with their back legs in the sand, on gravel beaches, or sometimes even in cultivated fields. They then lay between five to ten eggs in the pit, cover it, and then leave. In short, the eggs are abandoned. But what's interesting is that the sex of the offspring incubating in these eggs is determined, not by any predetermined process, but rather by temperature. During low-temperature incubations more males are hatched, while during high-temperature incubations more females hatch."

"What doess turtles eat, eh?" asked John Alex.

"Our turtle over there is an omnivore meaning that it eats plants and aquatic life. I have to qualify this however because it seems to depend upon the turtle's age. Younger turtles mostly eat aquatic life, I suppose you could call it 'meat', but older turtles chow down on quite a list of plants and aquatic life; from algae, duckweed and lily pads, to insects, slugs, leeches, tadpoles, fish eggs, frogs and even small fish."

"Sounds ta me thet turtles ain't too fussy 'bout what they eats. Somethin' like yerself Jin Alek."

"Speakin' a eatin', I could handle a couple a Jean's sandwiches 'bout now," said John Alex. "Ain't nothin' like food when yer hungry I always says."

Roddie turned and looked at Frugal. "Iss there anythin' other than Jin Alek here, thet kin kill an' eat a turtle? They're jist like little tanks."

"Yes they are, but turtles, especially young turtles, are killed and eaten by some bird species, snakes, skunks, and raccoons."

"Ya say young turtles, eh? How long does they live Frugal?"

"I guess it depends on a lot of things. Maximum ages vary, but are in the range of 35 years.

While the three of us were standing talking, Roddie had gone over to the pond, taken his boots, socks and pants off and waded out into the pond. He was quite a sight standing there in his old railroad cap, plaid shirt and polka-dot boxers.

John Alex chuckled. "Look it 'im, thin ass a toothpick on welfare. More meat on a Chinaman's whisker eh? Don't git yer banana hammock wet," he hollered.

Just then there was a shriek and wild thrashing out in the pond. Roddie was indeed lifting his legs high as he scrambled ashore.

He stood breathless and shaking at the edge of the pond. His polka-dotted banana hammock clinging like wet toilet paper to his thin hips.

"Jeede jumpin' Christopher!" he cried. "This gad damned monster leech wass 'bout ta lunge at me. Chased me right inta shore. I could feel the ferocious bugger snapin' at me arse all the way!"

When we finally stopped laughing we went over to the pond's edge. Soon we spotted Roddie's ferocious bugger looping complacently along, probably quite content in its little water world. It was about four inches long.

"Big monster, eh? Prob'ly make anaone throw a hissy." observed John Alex.

I looked at Frugal. "How about giving us a lesson on leeches."

"OK," said Frugal, still wiping the tears from his eyes.

"What do they like ta eat besides Roddie's scrawny arse, eh?" asked John Alex.

"Well," chuckled Frugal, "they *are* sanguivorous, which means that they're blood sucking parasites. These pond leeches parasitize turtles, frogs, fish, and ducks, but some will be attracted to humans. Especially those with shapely hairy legs and polka-dot boxers."

Perhaps Frugal didn't realize that this comment would now make him a target for Roddie. He had placed himself on a slippery slope indeed.

Roddie looked at him like you might look at a hair in your soup. But I *know* Roddie. Frugal had just done the right thing. He had begun to tease his friends. Now he would be accepted, but would be unmercifully teased, and would be expected to give as well as he got.

"Git on with yer lesson, ya font a misinformation."

"Oh, don't soil your see-through Stanfields," replied Frugal.

"At least with a wet tee shirt there's somethin' there ta see, eh?" Roddie chuckled. "Git on with it ya gommice."

"Yup, tell us yer story 'bout leeches, though I'd rather hev two er three a Jean's sandwiches, eh?"

Frugal smiled. "Ok, where were we? Let's talk about how they reproduce."

"Prob'ly not ass good a tale ass our walkin' set a gonads here could tell, but let's hear it," said Roddie.

I wondered who he was referring to, myself or John Alex.

"Leeches are actually hermaphroditic which means that they have both male and female sex organs."

"Some trees such as balsam fir, spruce and pine are also like this and are called monoecious," I interrupted. "A different name for the same thing."

Frugal nodded. "Yeah, that's true. Leeches have a clitellum, similar to earthworms. This clitellum is a thickened area in their skin. When a leech mates, it'll wrap its body around another leech and deposit its sperm on the clitellum of the leech that it's mating with. The other leech will do the same. The sperm will migrate to the ovaries. The clitellum secretes a jelly-like cocoon that holds the fertilized eggs. This cocoon is interesting, because it contains enough nutrients to feed the developing leeches and, although gelatinous, can even be eaten by a duck and pass unharmed through the duck's digestive system.

"Anyway, the cocoon is then shed from the adult leech and either buried at the bottom of the pond or attached to something underwater. Depending on a number of factors the little leeches will leave the cocoon in a month or two."

"So doess a leech hev a little Jimmy, eh?" asked John Alex.

Frugal looked at him vacantly. "Jimmy?"

"He means penis," I said.

"Oh. No it doesn't. The sperm is sharp and simply pushed through the skin by the intertwining bodies of the leeches."

"Doess ya effer think 'bout anathin' other than yer bladder, gut, an' Jimmy, Jin Alek?"

"Well, I often worries 'bout me asteroids, eh?"

"So how doess leeches suck blood?" asked Roddie.

"Well, let's assume that the little four inch 'monster' had been fast enough to catch Roddie and attach itself to his leg. The leech would bite, then make its body rigid. This would temporarily hold its sucker in place. In the meantime, it makes a tiny incision in the skin and excretes a mucous which helps the leech stick to the skin. Next the leech's saliva has an anticoagulant which enters the wound and permits the blood to flow freely and not clot. The leech would then relax its body and the blood would flow into it. It can consume several times its own weight of blood."

"What happens when the leech iss full?" asked Roddie, who kept checking his legs.

"It drops off. But because some anticoagulant remains, the

wound may take some time to finally stop oozing."

"Da ya thinks thet we should stop an' hev a cup a tea an' sandwich?" asked Roddie.

"Iss a pig's arse made outta pork?" smiled John Alex.

Roddie pulled on his pants, socks and boots and we headed back out the twisty trail to the truck.

We sat under some trees for lunch. Suddenly Roddie said, "Jin Alek, tell the boys 'bout the time ya bit yerself in the arse."

John Alex laughed, took a hearty swig of tea and said, "Wassn't thet a hoot? Not funny at the time though. I useta always take out me bottom denture an' carry it in me pocket. Jist installed it fer eatin'. Wal, one day I took it out an' absentmindedly put it in me back pocket. Didn't I slip on a wet root an' land squarely on me big fat arse. Needless ta say the teeth bit inta me an' I hev the scar ta prove it. I tells Martha thet it's me good luck horseshoe. She says that I probly jest gut hungry nuff ta try a bite, eh?"

"Martha's version sounds more like the truth ta me," chuckled Roddie.

We chatted back and forth then Roddie said, "I'd like ta take youse boys back ta the bog if'n ya gut time. Tain't far. What doess ya say?"

"Are there any snappin' buggers there Roddie?" asked Frugal.

"Er wet boxer contests, eh?" added John Alex.

Roddie turned and looked at me. "Tweedledee an' Tweedledum here would both hev ta think twice to qualify ass half-wits. Come on!"

The bog looked as a bog should look. This one was about ten acres in size. Around the edge were scattered spindly black spruce and tamarack, clumps of shrubs such as rhodora, wild raisin, false holly, kalmia (which some people call lambkill), Labrador tea and also cinnamon fern. As we walked out on the spongy sphagnum moss bog, the black spruce and tamarack got shorter and fewer. Some of the lower branches on the spruce were layering[*], so some of the spruce looked like a mother hen surrounded by a few baby chicks.

I pointed to a 5-foot (1.5 m) tall sickly-looking black spruce and asked Roddie how old he thought it was.

"I suspects thet it's older then it looks. Looks ta be 'bout eight er nine years so I'll say thet it's twenty-five."

Frugal fished a small hatchet from his ever present back pack, removed its edge protecting piece of garden hose, and handed me the axe. One good slanting swipe at moss level felled the tree. The annual growth rings were so close together on the cut stump that we couldn't count these rings to age the tree. I cut about a six-inch long piece off the bottom of the stem and put it in my vest pocket.

"I'll age this for you Roddie, but I'll need to do it back at the office using a microscope. I'll tell you its age the next time you're in."

"Yiss, yiss. How doess bogs git ta be bogs anaway?"

"What! Roddie I often thinks thet yer four cents short of a nickel, eh? Bogs wass always here. Thought at least ya knowed thet!"

"Well, that's not quite correct John Alex. Only about the bogs I mean. In this part of the world present-day bogs were once lakes that were depressions left after the glaciers retreated about 10,000 year ago."

"Really? How long ago wass thiss bog thet we're standin' on a lake, eh?"

"He jest told ya dipstick! 'Bout 10,000 years ago. An' ya subtlety infers thet *I'm* slow! So how doess bogs form anaway?"

"Let's start at the beginning then," I said.

"Humph! Ya always doess. It's back ta the earth coolin' agin Jin Alek,"

I smiled. "It all begins with a landlocked pond or lake. Since there's no water draining from the pond, this water becomes more acidic over time because rain picks up some carbon dioxide from the air as it falls, thus as I told you before, becoming a weak carbonic acid. Eventually some sedges and sphagnum moss begin to grow around the pond and out from its edges. The sphagnum also contributes acidity to the water."

"How doess thiss happen, it's jest a plant, eh?" said Roddie.

"True. But the sphagnum is able to draw minerals up from the bog. These are then exchanged for hydrogen ions thus making the bog more acidic."

"Two birds in the hand iss worth one in the bush, eh?" observed John Alex.

"In forest soils there are decomposer organisms such as bacteria and fungi. However, these don't function in cold, low oxygen and acidic conditions at the bottom of the pond. The result is an accumulation of dead plants along the pond or lake bottom. These dead plants can't decompose because of the unfavourable conditions for the decay organisms, so there's a gradual build up of fibrous, dead sphagnum which we call peat. Sphagnum is a neat plant because the top of the plant grows but the bottom dies and decays adding about a half an inch of height to the bog every twenty years. And so the peat layers grow until we have what we see today."

"How deep a pond er lake kin fill up with this here peat, eh?"

"I've seen rods pushed down through 23 feet (7 m) of peat before hitting the original lake bottom, but I read somewhere that some basins have peat more than 40 feet (12 m) deep.

"Let's walk further out into the bog, I'd like to show you a carnivorous plant."

As we walked, the sphagnum surface became even more spongy and floating under our feet. It almost felt that we were walking on a tippy raft.

"There it is. I pointed to a pitcher plant. Are you boys familiar with it?"

Roddie and John Alex both shook their heads.

"It's a native perennial herb that consumes insects, spiders, mites, snails, and even small frogs. Although these plants still photosynthesize, they have to consume critters to obtain nitrogen, phosphorus, vitamins and minerals because they're scarce in the sphagnum/peat."

"A plant thet eats animals? How doess thet work?" asked Roddie.

"Well, the plant develops a vertical vase-shaped leaf that can hold water. This pitcher partially fills with rainwater. On the leaf are red veins that lead down towards the bottom of the pitcher. These red veins are 'baited' by nectar glands and this lures the insect or prey down into the pitcher towards the water. However, if the prey changes its mind and wants to climb back out it's very difficult, because the tube is lined with fine downward-pointing hairs. As a result, the prey slides or falls into the water which contains a digestive enzyme that dissolves the unfortunate visitor thus turning the insect into nutrients for the plant's use."

"Jist like Jin Alek's big hairy gut kin dissolve Jacob Ming's doughnuts."

"Leave me big gut outta it. It costs money an' dedication ta maintain thiss emblem a healthy manhood, eh?"

"There's something that I'd like to add," said Frugal. There's the larvae of a small mosquito that actually lives in the digestive water of the plant. Unlike other insects that are digested by the enzymes, these larvae aren't harmed and live quite happily on the partially digested prey."

"Speakin' a digestion, I'd better be gettin' along before too long, eh. I gut ta take Martha ta town. We're goin' ta Ming's Ptomaine Palace fer taday's special. Martha calls it sushi but I makes Ming's pacemaker redline when I tells him I'll hev bait, eh."

As we slowly walked toward the edge of the bog, Roddie said, "Ya knows, once ya starts ta look inta how Nature works there's so much goin' on thet ya don't see, and kin neffer know unless ya looks, an' thinks, an' asks."

"So true," I said. "For example, take a close look at the needles on that spindly little spruce there." I handed him my 16x hand lens.

"I sees little white dots er tubes. What iss it?"

"It's a needle rust and the alternate host for it on spruce is the Labrador tea shrub."

"Thiss one here with the edges a the leaves curled down an' the brown furry underside?"

"Yep, thet's Labrador tea," said John Alex, "Martha gits me ta gather some once in a while so she kin put it in her drawers ta keep moths away, eh?"

Roddie and I smirked.

"Her *clothes drawers* ya uncultivated idjits!"

Frugal picked off a few leaves. "The leaves make a tasty tea. I like to pick them before the plant flowers and steep them in boiling water. But I wouldn't drink too much, because people tell me that an overdose might cause a splitting headache and one might even become slightly intoxicated."

"Cheap drunk, eh?"

"I read somewhere Frugal, that the species of Labrador tea

which grows in northern Europe has narcotic properties and is actually used by some German brewers to make their beer more intoxicating.

"You know, it's amazing when you stop and realize that all the things that we see around us are made up of different combinations of about a dozen elements and even more amazing that living things consist of four elements: carbon, hydrogen, oxygen and nitrogen.

"Take the wide variety of allelophatic chemicals for example. I took a short course on allelopathy once and, although I'd have to check my notes to give you the names of all those that I learned, some are alkaloids, benzoic acids, glycosides and tannins to name but a few. These are all different chemicals made by plants using the basic ingredients of sunlight, water and soil elements."

Roddie looked at John Alex, "Hear thet Jin Alek? Speaks what he believes ta be English."

"Yep, bet he kin even fart in Latin, eh?"

"Yiss, yiss. But I heard ya talkin' 'bout thiss allelopathy before. What iss it agin?"

"Allelopathy is the ability that some plants have to produce and release organic chemicals that either inhibit or stimulate the germination or growth of a different plant. Some common allelopathic plants include: black cherry, red pine, oaks, sugar maple, blueberry, aster, bracken fern, golden rod, lambkill, Labrador tea, and others."

"Stop the bus! Ya mentioned lambkill. Issn't thet the plant ya told us 'bout when we wass walkin' in? What did ya call it?"

"He told us thet it was kalmia, eh?"

"Yeah, that's right John Alex. Kalmia, or lambkill, is allelopathic to spruce. But not only that, kalmia also produces a toxic compound that makes the plant poisonous to livestock."

As we walked back out the trail to the trucks I asked Roddie if he thought that he had learned anything useful to tell his visiting grade-eight class.

"Yiss, yiss, I did. I'm goin' ta take them ta the pond and the bog and talk 'bout some a the stuff youse guys talked 'bout thiss mornin'. An' if there happens ta be a smart elliot in the group, I'll ask him ta wade out inta the pond. I jist hopes thet ferocious bugger iss still 'round an' gits him good.

"By the way, kin ya find out how old thet little tree is that ya cut without even askin' me permission? I'd like ta tell me class."

I said that I would.

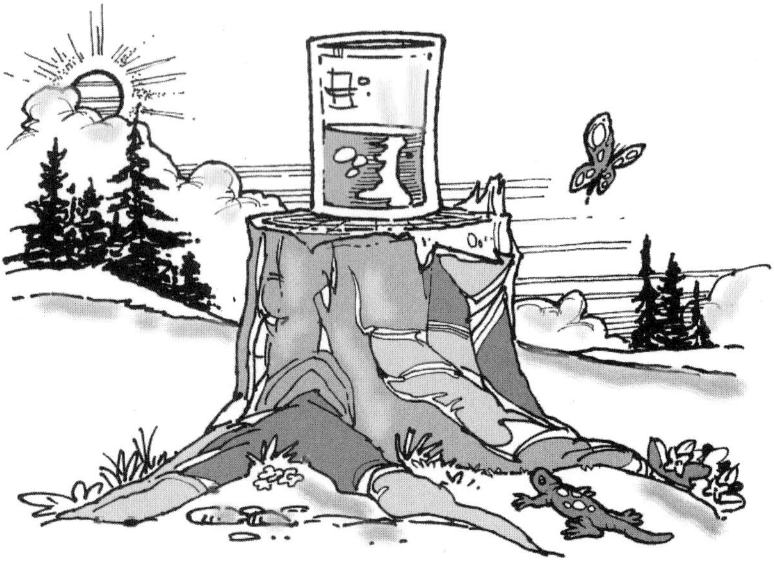

AN IDEALIST, A CYNIC, OR A REALIST?

What is not good for the beehive,
cannot be good for the bees.
—Marcus Aurelius

On Wednesday morning, I received a call from Ernie Boutlier asking me if I'd be one of the speakers at an annual meeting of forest practitioners. Ernie told me that the theme of this year's meeting was "Earth – Our Expanding Footprint and the Future."

I asked the usual questions of where, when, how much time I'd have, the availability of visual aids, who were the other speakers; and then said that I'd be happy to speak to the group.

I had three weeks to gather material for a topic that I was becoming more concerned about as the years passed. Now I'd be forced to explore this topic in detail. There's an old saying that there's nothing like the prospect of being hung in the morning to focus your mind. I got down to work.

I was scheduled to speak at 11:30, so on the morning of the presentation I arrived at the New Harbour Convention Centre at about 10:30. The room was crowded with a wide range of forestry people.

There were contractors, industry and private land foresters and forest technologists, biologists, and industrial sales representatives. I wondered what their response would be to my speech.

The moderator kept things on time so that at 11:30 I was told that, "The floor is yours."

I walked up to the podium, adjusted the mike, took a deep breath and began.

"Good morning, and thank you for the invitation. It's a privilege and indeed a pleasure to be part of your annual meeting.

"I've been asked to speak on how humans impact natural functions and processes. It's a rather timely topic considering the current public concern about the effects that climate change will have on the Earth as we know it today. And it's a rather alarming topic. Since I only have 30 minutes and lunch follows there probably won't be any opportunity for questions.

"I want you now to picture in your mind an upside down triangle. On the broad base of this inverted triangle imagine the word "public." Now come down your imaginary triangle about two thirds of the way and imagine the word "Nature's cycles." Then come to the very tip or point of your triangle. Imagine "forests and forestry" supporting this heavy inverted triangle. The three players in this imaginary triangle, the public, Nature's cycles, and forests are the topic of my speech.

"At 16 minutes past seven, eastern standard time on the evening of February 25, 2006 the world's population was expected to reach 6.5 billion people. This was according to the US Census Bureau's World Population Clock. They predict that the 7 billion threshold will be crossed in 2012.

"Stop and think, 6.5 billion people on spaceship Earth and more people coming with 4.1 birth's and 1.8 deaths every second. In this 30 minute presentation 7,380 babies will be born, 3,240 people will die, a net population gain of 4,140 in 30 minutes.

"Incidentally, the calculated sustainable human population for the Earth is about 2 billion people.

"And so the broad base of our inverted triangle is indeed getting crowded. How then is this population impacting Nature's functions and processes? To answer this, I suggest that we view the human impact by examining the following, and in so doing, I'll probably make some broad assumptions. We'll examine:

1. The North American population.
2. Its effect upon Nature's cycles.
3. The role of forests and forest professionals.

"By in large, we in North America are consumers and certainly not conservers. Not long ago I read that about 20 percent of the world's population lives here. But that we use more than 70 percent of the world's resources. In his novel *Ishmael*, Daniel Quinn wrote, "You're captives of a civilization system that more or less compels you to go on destroying the world in order to live."

"But how *do* we live? We just need to look around us here in New Harbour.

"Canada's average birth rate is 1.5 children per mother. But look at the enormous size of newly-constructed homes. Yet these are homes for smaller families. Look at urban sprawl, the migration of box stores and shopping centres with their huge parking lots to beyond the city core; look at the enormous garbage dumps which we like to call landfills. Areas which over time release noxious gases and toxic liquids to the environment.

"Or, reflect on the amount of land in North America that lies under asphalt; or the chemicals released into the air, soil, and water from our industries. Or the senseless destruction of war.

"The next time that you're in a coffee shop or fast-food restaurant, note that their cups and food containers are usually the "use and toss" type. While you're there, pick up a daily newspaper. Scan it carefully. Decide just how much of its information is something that *you* really should know.

"Here's a quote from John Vaillant's book *Golden Spruce*.

A highway logging truck can carry approximately 40 cubic metres.

It takes about 550 m^3 (nearly 14 truck loads) of wood to produce a week-end printing of the Globe and Mail, in addition to 13 million litres of water and 7.5 billion BTUs of energy.

"Perhaps you're thinking that 14 truck loads is no big deal. Maybe not. However, the amount of wood required to produce a Sunday edition of the New York Times *may* impress you, for it's almost twenty-five *thousand* cubic metres, which is 625 truckloads. Imagine 625 fully-loaded tractor trailers parked in a line along the highway. This line up of bumper to bumper trucks would be about 6.5 miles or 10.5 kilometres long. That's for *one* Sunday edition. If all the trucks were lined up for the Sunday Editions for one year, the line would be 338 miles (541 km) long. Now, consider the acreage that was cut to provide the wood for these trucks.

"On a brighter note, many people now recycle newspapers. However, perhaps those printed on recycled paper, which unfortunately requires using enormous amounts of de-inking chemicals, but still needs enormous amounts of water and energy, simply might not have a lot of important information. You be the judge.

"What about wetlands? A Natural Resources Canada report on Wetlands in 2004 states that since European settlement, wetland conversion to agriculture is estimated at over 20 million hectares. That's an area about 2.7 times *larger* than New Brunswick. But you and I in this room, know that wetlands are Nature's "kidneys" because of their ability to trap, filter and neutralize sewage and toxic wastes. In short, wetlands help to purify water. Many people complain about paying $1.00 for a litre of gasoline; yet willingly pay more for the same volume of water. What's wrong with our water? Could it be our impact upon Nature?

"Just what *are* the human impacts upon Nature? First we must remember that we do indeed live on a self-contained spaceship that's surrounded by a protective atmosphere. This spaceship can't dock anywhere to take on supplies; what it carries must last until the end of the journey. Nature ensures that this is possible by recycling everything. There's no such thing as waste in Nature. That term is a human invention.

"Let's briefly examine four cycles in Nature and see how they're disturbed by human activity. These cycles are the hydrologic cycle, carbon cycle, nitrogen cycle, and sulphur cycle.

"Humans interfere with the hydrologic cycle in three ways. First, because of our sheer numbers (6.5 billion) we daily remove vast quantities of fresh water from ground water, rivers, and lakes. Second, we contaminate water. Water is often used as a carrier for the disposal of chemicals and wastes. The all too familiar "solution by dilution." Also, as I mentioned previously, we infill or drain wetlands. The third way is by deforestation. Following deforestation water runs off quickly and no longer infiltrates the soil to recharge groundwater supplies. In fact, urban planners pride themselves on their ability to efficiently get rid of water.

"The second cycle that we interfere with is the carbon cycle. We use vast quantities of fossil fuels to generate heat and energy. This, plus escalating global deforestation and other human-caused emissions, has increased the carbon dioxide in the atmosphere by about 25 percent between 1870 and 1990. As you know, too much carbon dioxide in the atmosphere is one of the reasons for climate change. This, in turn, will have many long-term effects on insect, plant, animal, and human life.

"Next comes the nitrogen cycle. When fuels are burned, one of the compounds released is nitrogen oxide. This gas combines with atmospheric oxygen to form a greenhouse gas called nitrogen dioxide. Nitrogen dioxide breaks down the ozone layer. I'm sure you're all aware that when the ozone layer is broken down there's an increase in animal and human skin cancers. But nitrogen dioxide also does something else. It reacts with hydrogen in the atmosphere to form nitric acid. This falls to Earth damaging marine and plant life.

"And, although there are many other cycles, the last one that we'll examine today is the sulphur cycle. Sulphur compounds, such as sulphur dioxide, hydrogen sulphide, and sulphuric acid, are formed and emitted into the atmosphere during coal burning, the refining of petroleum products, and the smelting processes. These compounds then fall back to Earth and cause soils and water to become more acidic. As a result, some lakes have become so acidic that they are now barren of all life.

"We've now made our way down the inverted triangle to its point, forests and forestry, which happens also to be the point of 'our' being here today.

"I recently heard a CBC report which stated that forestry is being considered by some as a "sunset industry." I beg to differ, but *will* agree that forestry, as we know it today, will change. There are now immense pressures on forests and forestry. As a result of globalization and an ever-shrinking forest land-base we now have serious problems. But in my view we haven't seen anything yet, for I believe that within the next decade there will be dramatic changes in how forests are managed. Whether managed for fiber, carbon, or other values.

"Forests in our region are just beginning to feel the effects of a warming climate. We don't know how much the average temperature will change in the next 50 years. But temperature changes from 1° to 6° Celsius have been modelled. And the results are indeed sobering As you've probably all heard, we can expect more severe storms more often, rising sea levels, an increase in insects (+2° may mean one to five new insect families), an increase in diseases; some temperature-stressed native tree species such as balsam fir will not survive, (+2° may also mean a 600 kilometre northward movement of tree species); and there will be more intense and severe wildfires.

"So where do forests now stand in this glum scenario? In 1851, Henry David Thoreau wrote, "Wildness is the preservation of the world." He was correct but at that time he didn't have to consider over-population, pollution, rampant consumption, or that wild card called climate change. We now do. Have these pressures pushed Nature too far? Can they be fixed? I don't know these answers. But I *do* know that *healthy* forests are indeed one of the main components necessary to maintain a sustainable spaceship. And I *do* know, with one provision, that forest professionals are the only people specifically trained in the many aspects of forest management including fish, wildlife, soils, and forest health issues. That provision is that these forestry professionals must have access to, and understand, the most current available research.

"However, we still have much to learn about ecological systems and processes in the Acadian forest. With research this can be done. The implementation of the research results may be more difficult, for a more ecological method of forest management could have significant economic and social impacts. But so could doing nothing.

"Perhaps forestry can be likened to a bus driving through time. Over the years it has been driven faster and faster. It's been over many rough roads, and has been repaired and modified many times. The bus called forestry is now approaching an important intersection. At this intersection, one road sign points to a place called Decline. The other points to a place called Restoration. The road to Decline is straight and smooth. However, the road to Restoration is bumpy and still under construction. Which road should the bus take? *Who* is driving the bus?

"Forest professionals *must* step up to the plate, *must* become more vocal, and *must assume* a leading role in the decision making and implementation of a changed forestry.

"If not you, who? If not now, when?

"In closing, I'll leave you with what I call "Ten Understandings" that I suggest forestry professionals should think about.

- We must understand the importance that forests play in the health of the Earth.
- We must understand that it wasn't forestry that created the current environmental conditions.
- We must understand that humans are a part of Nature. We are but one species among many.
- We must understand, to the best of our ability, how Nature works.
- We must understand that one person will never know it all, we must work as teams to be effective.
- We must understand that continued forestry and ecological research and technical transfer are necessary.
- We must understand the need to restore or renew forests so that they again become ecologically healthy.
- We must understand that we must assume a greater role in educating children and the public in appreciating Nature and in adopting a land-use ethic.
- We must understand that the public must develop a greater consumer ethic when it comes to using forest products.
  And finally:
- We must understand that we'll meet opposition.

"Present-day forests may be thought of as a glass half full of water sitting on a freshly-cut stump. Will the water level in the glass continue to lower? Or, will we, as forest professionals, continually top up the water in the glass? In my view those are our options. It will take our understanding and commitment. What do *you* think?

"Thank you for your attention, I hope that I've given you something to reflect upon as our bus called forestry travels into the future."

There was polite clapping as I returned to my seat. I knew that I had rubbed some of the group the wrong way. And I understood. They were probably focusing on the loss of jobs. Thus, the thought of a significant change in forest practices was disturbing, to say the least. We all tend to react this way when our long-term beliefs and even the means of our livelihood are questioned or perhaps threatened.

However, I believe that the forest should not only have a timber value, but also many other values such as biochemicals, medicinals, pharmaceuticals, recreation, aesthetic and spiritual values, wildlife, maple products, mushrooms, and let's not forget oxygen production, carbon sequestration, flood and erosion protection, and water purification and storage. Yes, I thought, we *need* wood, but we must be smarter in getting and using it efficiently.

Since I had an afternoon appointment with a landowner, I had to leave the meeting early. As I drove back to Big Spoon Cove I couldn't help but reflect on a quote by Sydney Harris: "An idealist believes the short run doesn't count. A cynic believes the long term doesn't matter. A realist believes what is done or left undone in the short run determines the long run."

I concluded that perhaps I was a realist, but perhaps I'd be more popular with some forestry people if I was a cynic.

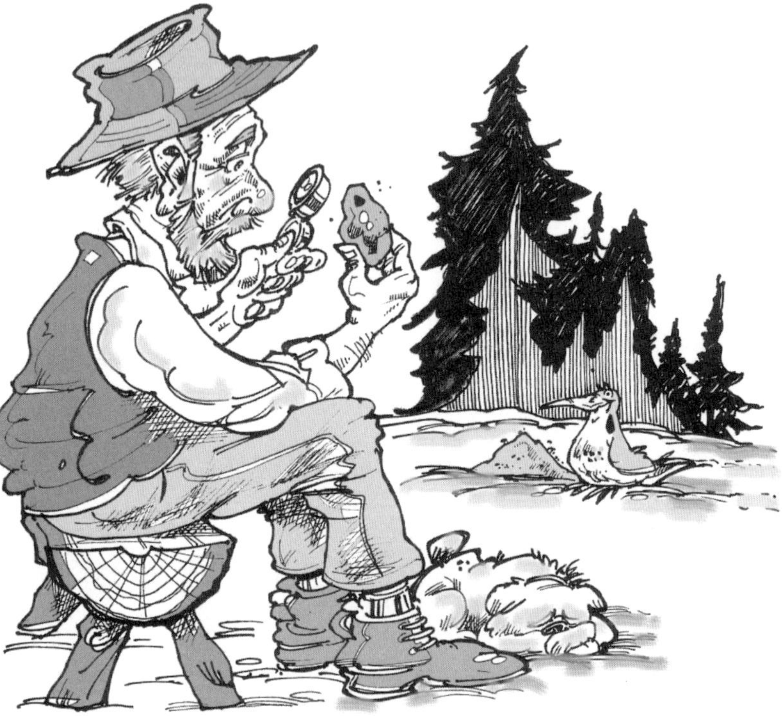

MUSINGS WHILE WALKING WITH A HERMIT

Primum non nocere
(First, do no harm)
- Unknown

Brother Thomas and his new little pug dog met me on the trail into his cabin. Brother Thomas doesn't look like our normal perception of a Trappist monk/hermit who lives alone in his little hermitage in the woods. He was dressed in a dark green shirt and pants, a battered green Tilley hat, and he now sported a neatly trimmed white beard. He would easily be passed by on the street as just another citizen of Big Spoon Cove. Except for his eyes. They were an illuminous blue that shone with intelligence and curiosity. Brother Thomas missed very little.

I had to first be introduced to the little tan and black pug that was vigorously sniffing at my pant leg.

"This is Dr. Watson."

"Why did you pick *that* name?" I asked.

Brother Thomas smiled. "After I got him I didn't name him for a few weeks. Just couldn't come up with a name that seemed to suit him. And then I noticed how curious he was, always sniffing and exploring for clues around the cabin and woods, and how he would seem to sit and 'ponder'. Hence the name. Believe it or not, Dr. Watson has helped me sharpen my observation skills. He likes to sniff out things in the woods and then stand back waiting for me to get down on my knees for a closer look. He's a great companion, as was his namesake I guess."

Brother Thomas looked at me, "Got time for a little stroll in the woods?"

"Has a Catholic priest ever heard of the Pope?" For obvious reasons, I didn't use John Alex's saying, "Iss a pig's arse made outta pork?"

"Good. Let's go. I have some questions for you."

"And I have some for you." I said.

Brother Thomas had recently finished cutting about a kilometre-long trail through the monastery woodlot. He said that he used this trail for meditative walks, exercise, and just being close to Nature.

Dr. Watson trundled ahead on his little bowed legs, occasionally stopping for a quick pee as the monk and I walked silently along the trail.

Brother Thomas stopped and looked around. He pointed to some large dead standing aspens and then to a few good-sized balsam firs which had broken off and now lay on the forest floor.

"Is this cause for concern?"

"Do you want a wood utilization, or an ecological answer?" I asked.

"Both, you know me."

"From an economic viewpoint the aspen and balsam fir were overmature and aren't worth much now. These are two relatively short-lived species that must be harvested earlier than other longer-lived species such as spruce, white pine, yellow birch or sugar maple.

"But from an ecological point of view, these standing dead trees which are called snags and these downed trees are very valuable because of what they give back to the site. You know, there's much more mass of living organisms and tissue in a dead tree than in an alive and apparently healthy tree."

"You're saying that there's more life in a dead tree than a living tree? Are you serious?"

"Let's begin with snags, because this is where the decay process usually begins. Broken limbs or tops allow the entrance of decay organisms. This decay can gradually migrate into and down the tree trunk.

"Another cause of tree death is from various root and heart rots which slowly migrate from the base of the tree upwards in the heartwood."

We walked over to examine a fallen balsam fir. Its heartwood was riddled with ant galleries and passageways. The exterior of the trunk had numerous woodpecker holes.

"Did the ants kill this tree?" asked Brother Thomas.

"No. Contrary to what many people think, the black or carpenter ants don't eat the deteriorating wood that they remove while building their nesting site, however they'll often extend their galleries into adjacent sound wood. The ants feed on other insects, plant juices and honeydew from aphids."

"Honeydew? Obviously you don't mean honeydew melons. Please explain."

"Honeydew is a sticky, sugary excretion from aphids and some scale insects that feed on plant sap. Black and red ants feed on this high energy source and even protect the aphids from predators such as lady beetles. The ants either lap up the secretions from where they landed on the plant leaves or bark or actually "milk" the aphid to encourage excretion by rubbing the aphid with their antenna, thereby causing the feeding aphid to excrete a drop of honeydew. Unconsumed honeydew on leaves and bark can cause the growth of a black fungus known as black sooty mold which may interfere with the plant's metabolism. So ants actually help to keep the plant or tree 'clean'."

"What's the story on these large holes?"

"As you can see, they're rectangular in shape, so they were excavated by a pileated woodpecker. They're the largest woodpecker that we have in this region. A beautiful bird, I'd say about 16 inches (40 cm) long. They're nice to see; remind me of a prehistoric pterodactyle when they're flying."

"I've never noticed one, are they common?"

I thought about it. "I guess I'd say they're common in older softwood and hardwood forests or even in younger forests as long as there are some snags left in it. A pileated needs a forested territory of 100 to 200 acres (40 to 80 ha). So large clearcuts often significantly reduce available areas. I'm not sure what effect this has on the pileated population."

"Where do they nest?" asked Brother Thomas.

"In large old cavity trees. They'll make a round or vertically elliptical nesting hole quite high in the tree. What we see here on these downed balsam firs are called feeding holes. The bird likes an old rotting tree or stump. It'll perch on the side of it and listen for inside insect activity. If it hears movement it'll excavate a hole, then flick in its long, sticky, barbed tongue and snatch the ants.

"Pileateds are an important bird in Nature because there are probably more than 50 other species that use and indeed depend on the holes made by this big woodpecker."

"Name some so that I can watch for them."

"Around the lake watch for wood duck, merganser, and tree swallow nest holes, in deeper old growth forest areas look for owl or flying-squirrel nests, and out by your cabin you may have black-capped chickadees or red-breasted nuthatches nesting in old woodpecker holes."

"That reminds me. The other day when I was walking over from the monastery I noticed a fairly big brown bird fly away from me. It was on the ground near the edge of the woods. I went over to see what it was doing and it was apparently probing at an anthill. Any idea what kind of a bird that was?"

"Did it show a lot of white feathers to you as it flew away?" I asked.

"Yes it did."

"Sounds like a northern flicker. It's a medium-sized woodpecker and its main food is insects. Mound ants probably make up nearly half its diet. An interesting fact about flickers is that they use the acid which ants produce to preen their feathers and deter parasites. You sometimes see some other birds dusting themselves in ant hills for the same reason.

"What kind of acid?"

"Formic acid. It's fairly common in Nature. For instance it's found in stinging nettles and the stings of many insects including bees and ants. The ants use it as a chemical defence and also as a herbicide to kill any vegetation that shades their ant hill. And you know what? Formic acid is also used to synthesize the artificial sweetener called aspartame."

"My, my," said Brother Thomas. "Think I'll stick to honey, no pun intended.

"You talked about snags, so what's the story on downed trees and rotting logs and stumps?"

"Downed woody material laying on the forest floor becomes very wet inside. During warm weather this wet wood is an ideal condition for mycorrhizal fungi growth and also for the growth of nitrogen-fixing bacteria. It's important to realize that decomposing wood actually provides a steady, slow release of nitrogen which can be used later by plants and trees. Through time the downed wood slowly decays and is utilized by fungi, lichens, invertebrates, mosses, plant roots, seedlings trees, amphibians, and small mammals. In fact, about 40% of woodland wildlife depends on dead wood. In my view, rotting wood is a critical part of a healthy forest. But many forest ecosystems are currently suffering because of management techniques whereby the ratio of living to dead wood has been significantly altered."

Brother Thomas nodded, "For dust thou art, and unto dust thou shalt return. I guess the author of Genesis wasn't only referring to humans."

"True. Do you know Matthew, the guy that turns bowls? Big tall fellow? Lives in that log house by the stream on Foxbrook Road?"

Brother Thomas shook his head. "Don't think I've ever met him, but I've seen one of his bowls. Beautiful."

"They are. Matthew uses spalted wood for many of his bowls. Spalting is actually the decomposing or rotting process that we were just talking about. The spreading fungi and microbe deposits induce chemical reactions which results in artistic black or multicoloured streaks in the wood. Light coloured woods such as birch, beech and maple spalt nicely. So Matthew turns these on his lathe and the bowls are each one of a kind with a unique pattern of lines, streaks and colours."

Brother Thomas frowned. "But, if the wood is rotting will the bowls last? Won't they continue to rot as bowls?"

"No. The spalting process can be stopped once the wood is dried. Remember I said that rotting wood requires warm weather and wet wood?"

Brother Thomas nodded.

"Well, to be more precise, the wood moisture content must be above 25% and the temperature between 60º and 80º Fahrenheit for spalting to occur. Once the wood has been dried the fungi can't grow, so the spalting stops. The trick is to stop the spread of fungi before the wood becomes too soft and punky to turn on the lathe.

"There is one precaution though. Matthew told me that spalted wood may still contain spores and there's medical evidence that serious lung diseases have been traced to fungi found in rotting wood. For this reason he always wears a dust mask when working with this wood."

We had been standing talking next to the fallen balsam fir for some time. Dr. Watson whined his displeasure at our inactivity so we took the hint and moved on.

"I sometimes let him think he's boss," smiled Brother Thomas.

"Sometimes?" I smiled.

As we walked along, Brother Thomas told me how he used to work in the monastery's carpenter shop and made things using white pine. He said that some of the boards were clear, some had blue colouring while some had dark brown markings. He asked why.

"Stains in wood are caused by a number of things such as fungi, microorganisms, and chemical reactions. The blue stain in white pine is caused by the growth of dark-coloured fungi which can grow if the pine is cut in the summer and the logs are left on the ground for a few days. Brown stain, often called coffee-brown stain, is also caused by a fungus and the concentration and oxidation of extractive chemicals while the wood is in storage.

"There's another stain that occurs in hardwoods called mineral stain. It can colour the wood olive to greenish-black to brown. I'm not sure how this stain develops but I suspect that it's a chemical reaction in the wood."

Part way up the hill Brother Thomas pointed to a large partially rotted stump. It was about three feet in diameter.

"That was once a nice pine tree," he said.

"Sorry, it was a hemlock," I replied.

"How do you know, you didn't examine it very closely?"

I pointed. "See that reddish brown fungus on the side of the stump? It's called a hemlock varnish shelf, and it's a good way to identify an old hemlock stump."

As we walked slowly on, I asked Brother Thomas what he was reading.

"I've recently read a marvelous book called, *What Remains To Be*

Discovered, about the wonder of cells," he replied. "Perhaps I should be more specific, living cells, not jail cells. Anyway, the book was fascinating. The author, John Maddox, explored how cells differed from one another in a multi-celled organism. He pointed out the remarkable difference between a nerve cell, a skin cell, a bone cell and a blood cell. Yet miraculously, these diverse cells all developed from a single fertilized egg. And I thought of you when I read about the magic in a single fertilized egg hatching into a caterpillar, then the chrysalis in which it changes into a butterfly. It's truly amazing that DNA in the fertile cell doesn't only specify the types of cells that eventually develop, but is in fact a recipe that guides the development from embryo to adult."

"I call that pretty neat," I said.

"I call it Divine Intelligence," said Brother Thomas, "But then, you could say that I have a bias."

About half way around the trail Brother Thomas had built a log bench and he suggested that we sit and talk for a while. That seemed like a good idea to Dr. Watson for he promptly lay on his belly with his tongue out and panted loudly.

The bench overlooked a ravine. I suppose it was about 30 feet (9 m) deep. On both sides of the steep slopes were large red spruce, hemlock, white pine, sugar maple and yellow birch. A rocky brook about 12 feet (3.6 m) wide tumbled along at the bottom.

It was peaceful sitting there listening to the brook and the wind whispering through the pines, even though the stillness was soon punctuated by Dr. Watson's snoring.

Brother Thomas turned to me while digging in his pants pocket. "I found this one day and brought it with me today to show you." He passed it to me.

"It's a piece of petrified wood," I said.

"Yes, I know, but how did it become petrified and how old is it? You're not getting off the hook that easy."

"I guess there really aren't any accidents in this perfect universe,"

I said. "Just last week I took a piece of petrified wood over to Dr. Turcotte, a retired geology professor living in Northport and asked him the same questions. Let's see if I can regurgitate his answers for you. He told me the word 'petrify' means to turn to stone. So petrified wood means wood that has turned into stone. It's actually the fossil of a woody plant preserved by what they call permineralization. This means the addition of minerals into spaces in an organic structure that eventually results in a fossil. Here's how Dr. Turcotte explained the process to me.

"Since oxygen causes rotting of all materials, wood which eventually is to become petrified must be excluded from oxygen to prohibit its decay. This could happen if the tree tipped into a river and was quickly buried by silt. If petrification is to take place, minerals from the water are deposited in the now water-filled cells in the wood. This is, as I said, permineralization, and these minerals might eventually replace the wood's cellular structure. Dr. Turcott stressed that this process of mineral replacement is extremely slow, taking millions of years."

"Did he mention what minerals are found in petrified wood?"

"Yes, he did. He said that silicon dioxide is the most common replacement mineral. The piece of petrified wood that I showed him had brown streaks, which he said were iron oxides; white areas, which he identified as silicates of aluminum; and black areas, which he told me could be either manganese oxides or carbon. He thought mine was carbon."

Brother Thomas carefully examined his piece of petrified wood using my hand lens. "Mine doesn't have any white colour, but there's a faint trace of green. Did your geologist tell you what a green colour means?"

"Yes, green indicates copper, cobalt, or chromium."

"Isn't it amazing! I'm actually holding in my hand a piece of what was once a living tree that grew millions of years ago. Reminds me of a favourite quote by Thomas Huxley, 'For every man the world is as fresh as it was at the very first day, and as full of untold novelties for him who has the eyes to see them.' And also of another quote by Saint Bernard, 'Trees and stones will teach thee more than thou can learn from the mouth of a magister'.

"Now, when we met today you said you had a question for me. Let's hear it."

"It took me a minute to remember what I was going to ask him. His Huxley quote reminded me.

"My wife recently bought a book on meditation. It outlines a simple way to still your mind and details the physical and mental benefits to be had by regularly practicing it for about 30 minutes a day. Of course I had to read the book too. Anyhow, in it the author wrote that meditation actually opens the doors of our perception wider. I know that you meditate, so do you perceive things clearer?"

He smiled. "I'll give you the short answer and then offer my help to you and your wife. The short answer is yes. Any experience that stills your mind is beneficial and can be called meditation. However, there are formal methods in every spiritual tradition, but the overall purpose is the same for everyone. The meditator gradually becomes more able to focus his or her mind and thus becomes more aware.

"Now, here's my offer. I believe that it's much better to be taught meditation by someone who meditates and can answer any questions that you two will undoubtedly have, rather than trying to learn how from a book. Speak to your wife and if you folks want to learn I'll be happy to teach you."

While we were sitting chatting the sky had clouded over and it began to, as Roddie says, "spit" rain. Brother Thomas whistled to the sleeping pug and we slowly made our way back to his hermitage.

As we said our goodbyes, Brother Thomas grinned. "Here's one for the road...something to ponder as you drive back home. I read this in Louise Young's book *The Unfinished Universe*. It's about a human egg and sperm. We know that a male sperm contains a single strand of nucleic acid and enough protein to encase it. The female egg however, is much larger, and contains many proteins in solution, enzymes, other chemicals, and a single strand of nucleic acid. When the sperm and egg fuse the complete information for making a finished human is created. Think about it, all the cell structures and functions, facial features, skin and hair colour… everything is mapped out at that moment of conception. As you would say, "pretty neat, what?"

"Indeed."

THE PAST, THE PRESENT, AND THE FUTURE

> *If I were to prescribe one process in the training of men* (or women) *which is fundamental to success in any direction, it would be thorough training in the habit of observation. It is a habit which every one of us should be seeking ever more to perfect.*
> - Eugene G. Grace

I know Roddie will be disappointed when I tell him that I had spent a day alone walking over his new woodlot. Quite frankly, I needed to be alone to keep track of distances, to observe, to take notes, and to think. I also know that Roddie and I will explore it together sometime soon.

The ability to be a keen observer is an unwritten job requirement for anyone working in resource management. Mistakenly, most people think they're good observers. They're not. And it's not really their fault, because our brains are 'wired up' to prevent us from being overwhelmed by an overload of stimuli. Think of all the things you *saw* this morning as you drove to work. The houses you passed. The vehicles you passed or passed you. The species of trees you passed.

Or, we all use touch-tone phones daily, so what letters of the alphabet are missing on the key pad? What's the image on the back of a twenty-dollar bill? What's the colour of your vehicle's license sticker? What was your partner wearing this morning?

Don't feel too bad if you don't know the answers. People typically don't. However, you *have seen* all these things, and your brain chose to consider them as unnecessary. *It* and not *you*, decided what you should perceive. So if observation skill is that important, can it be improved, and if so, how? Fortunately it's not that difficult. Here's one simple way that, if used, soon becomes a habit. A good habit – that allows you to actually see and not 'overlook' what you're observing.

Perhaps it would be easier to remember if we gave it an acronym. How about something like TBA. This usually means 'to be announced' but for our purpose it'll mean 'top-bottom-around'. By using this method you force yourself to not only look *at* things, but to systematically look *for* things. Things which should be there, and conversely, things that shouldn't be there. This systematic method may be used to describe anything; from a person standing in front of you, to a single tree, to a stand of trees. For example, here are the areas you would observe when describing a softwood tree using the TBA method. I'll list it in tabular form beginning at the top of the tree, coming down its bole *, then looking around the tree and examining the soil it's standing upon. (Remember, terms with an asterisk are defined in the Glossary at the back of the book).

STAND	SITE COVER
Species*	Snags*
Height	Downed woody material*
Crown*	Dens/Nests*
Insects/Disease	Shrubs
Cone crop	Ericaceous vegetation*
Limbyness*	Herbaceous vegetation*
Taper*	Ribes/Rubes*
Diameter*	Surface rock
Previous stem damage*	Watercourse
Age*	
REGENERATION	**SITE/SOIL**
Species	Topography*
Height	Exposure*
Age	Aspect*
Distribution*	Duff thickness*
Stocking*	Soil texture*
Vigor*	Rocks
Insects/Disease	Rooting depth*
	Drainage*

Last week I received aerial photos showing Roddie's new woodlot. These photos were taken eight years ago and showed most of the lot covered by a canopy of softwood, mixedwood and hardwood stands. I placed two adjacent photos side by side and, peering through a stereoscope, soon had portions of his lot in three dimension. I could now see the hills, hollows and watercourses. And if I looked carefully, I could observe traces where the boundary lines had previously been brushed out. From this I was able to draw the woodlot's boundaries on the photos.

Next, I took an ink pen which drew a fine line and, looking through the stereoscope*, delineated the stands. This simply means drawing a line around the perimeter of the stands. This allowed me to eventually determine the stand size and also gave me an idea of where I wanted to visit rather, than wandering aimlessly over the lot.

The pre-cut stands were relatively large. I jotted down the stand type* and determined the size of the stand using a dot grid*. When finished, I sat back and reviewed my notes.

Stand #	Stand Type	Area (ac.)	Area (ha)
1	Gravel pit	5.0	2.02
2	Bog	10.0	4.05
3	Pond	3.0	1.21
4	Softwood	20.0	8.09
5	Hardwood	30.0	12.15
6	Mixedwood	15.0	6.07
7	Softwood	10.0	4.05
8	Recent burn	7.0	2.83
Total		100.0	40.47

I now wanted to find a point on the photo that I could also find when I visited the woodlot. I focused on the bog. On the photo it looked like a perfect oval, but on the western edge of the bog I thought that I could see a rock outcrop. This would be my starting point.

I drew a line from this rock outcrop to the center of stand ④. Then from ④ to the center of the five previously forested stands that I wanted to visit. I continued doing this until I had drawn a 'dog leg' cruise line to the five stands. Stand ⑧, the old burn, appeared to be near a massive white pine, so I should end up somewhere near it, or its stump. I then calculated the azimuth*, measured the lengths of the lines and was now ready to head out early the next morning to spend a day in the woods. Alone. As Brother Thomas would say, "Good for the soul!"

I remember that I was just about to go for a cup of tea when I received a phone call from Mrs. Major. Hearing her voice, I immediately did a hemorrhoidal clutch. Maintaining her image, she spoke in capital letters and immediately came to the point.

"I have a question. As you may or may not know we have two bird feeders here at the school so the children can see different birds. Don McCarthy, one of our teachers, said we shouldn't be feeding birds in the spring. Is he right?

Gosh, she was even intimidating on the phone. "You should really be asking our wildlife biologist, Fruellen MacDougal this, but he's in Fredericton, so I'll tell you what I do. I feed chickadees, finches, nuthatches, juncos, bluejays etc. during the winter, spring, and early summer, and hummingbirds from spring through to fall.

"However, whether or not you feed year-round is a personal decision. I like to feed in the spring because it attracts birds that are migrating north to their breeding grounds, and feed in early summer because birds need added energy for their rapidly growing nestlings."

"Thank you." She immediately hung up.

Well, I thought, that was short and sweet. Perhaps the war surplus salesman dropped in with a shipment of army boots. That, or she needed to pee.

By 6:30 the next morning I was standing at the rock outcrop at the eastern edge of Roddie's bog. What a day! Not a cloud in the sky, bird's chirping, and enough breeze to keep the blackflies at bay, temporarily anyway.

I set the azimuth on my compass, sighted and began counting my paces * as I headed for point ④. On the aerial photo, point ④ was in the center of a softwood stand. Since then, the stand had been cut. I was soon stepping over ruts, walking through scattered grass and raspberries and wading through heavy brown slash. White spruce limbs and tops were strewn over the ground.

As I slowly paced the distance to point ④ I carefully looked around. When I got to the point I stuck my walking stick in the ground and wandered around a bit. There were just a few scattered cones on the limbs so it hadn't been a heavy seed year when the stand was clearcut. I examined stumps. The average stump diameter was about 10 inches (25 cm), and by counting the growth rings on some stumps, I found the average age to be 49 years. The stumps were sound and the growth rings showed consistently good growth. The last growth ring next to the bark was complete, and so it, and the heavy rutting suggested that the stand was cut the fall before last.

Apart from some scattered balsam fir regeneration that wasn't broken, I couldn't find any white spruce seedlings or germinants. Curious, I aged some of the three-foot (0.9 m) tall fir. They were about 35 years old and certainly didn't have enough time left in their short life span in this county to develop into much of a tree.

The ground under the slash* lacked the usual humps and hollows that develop on the forest floor as trees either die and eventually fall, are broken off by wind, or uprooted by heavy winds. As these trees slowly decompose and turn into soil the result is an undulating terrain known as mound and pit topography. However, when the site is relatively smooth and there's little evidence of mounds and pits it usually means that it was once used for agriculture, and that it was probably an old field which, in this case grew up in white spruce.

To confirm my suspicion I pulled the folding army-surplus shovel from my pack and dug a small soil pit down through the duff and soil to the hard 'C' horizon, called by some the parent material. I then looked at the side of the soil pit. Sure enough, there as no 'A' horizon; a reasonable indication that the soil had been previously mixed by ploughing. From the bottom of the duff to the 'C' horizon was about 14 inches (36 cm) and there were no signs of mottling or a compacted subsoil. Mottles are small spots or blotches that are usually orange-red in colour and, depending on their abundance and distance up from the 'C' horizon, indicate imperfect or poor drainage. I was checking for a compacted subsoil or, as it's called, a plow pan, because repeated agricultural plowing sometimes caused the formation of a hard layer which young tree roots have difficulty penetrating.

Thus far, this single pit indicated a deep, well-drained soil. This type of old field stand doesn't easily regenerate to similar species following a disturbance so I suspected that Roddie might want to plant this area. If so more pits would eventually be dug around the site to confirm this. However, this was enough for my initial walk-about.

I next picked up a handful of soil from the face of the small pit to determine its texture. The soil was a sandy loam. This quick, simple field assessment consists of moist cast, ribbon, feel, and shine tests. For more information on this and other site factors, see Appendix A.

I made a few notes, set the azimuth on my compass and started pacing toward point ⑤. As I reached the edge of the previous softwood stand I stepped across a moss-covered stone fence and started up a slight grade. I was now in what was the hardwood stand* before it was cut.

There was no slash or tops, just short scattered raspberry canes, so walking was easy. As I paced I looked at the stumps. The pre-cut stand species were primarily sugar maple, beech, yellow birch, red maple, plus scattered hemlock and red spruce. Everything had been cut.

When I reached the top of the hill, I came upon a rectangular depression. It was about 20' x 20' (6 m x 6 m) and perhaps 5' (1.5 m) deep. A large recently-cut red spruce stump was perched part way down the side of the depression. I jotted down the distance that I'd paced, stuck my walking stick in the ground and stepped down into the depression. It looked like an old cellar excavation. I went over, bent, and counted the growth rings from the pith * to the bark on the cut stump. The stump was about 219 years old.

"Wow," I murmured. "This old cellar must have been dug by an early settler. I must tell Stanley Farquer about this." (I admit it, I often talk out loud to myself when alone in the woods). Anyhow, Stanley had moved to the Big Spoon Cove area a number of years ago and soon became interested in local history. He had even bought a metal detector and was apparently finding some buried artifacts around long-abandoned farms.

I resumed pacing and soon reached the center of stand ⑤. I again stuck my walking stick in the ground to mark the point and then wandered around. The absence of slash indicated that the trees had been cut and taken to roadside, limbs and all. This makes economic sense. It's efficient. It's maximum utilization. However, from an ecological viewpoint it's harmful because long-term site productivity is reduced. Elements such as nitrogen, potassium and magnesium are mainly concentrated in the foliage, while calcium is contained in the limbs and bark. By removing them, the site is actually robbed of these necessary recyclable elements.

I got down on my knees and aged several stumps and found that there were at least four age classes.* This told me that this used to be an uneven-aged,* shade-tolerant stand that had been clearcut. Darn! In my view there are better ways to manage this type of stand.

I looked around for regeneration. There were tiny sugar maple germinants* that probably wouldn't survive a hot summer; scattered stump sprouts* on only the smaller-diameter sugar maple and yellow birch stumps, abundant sprouting on the red maple and beech stumps, and abundant beech root suckers.*

Off to my right I saw what must have once been a nice little spring. It was now a muddy skidder wheel rut, but the water had cleared and was again bubbling up from deep underground.

The trees had been cut quite close to the ground. This was good because the lower root-collar* sprouts would grow from the stump in a "J" shape as opposed to the more unstable and rot-prone "V" shape which often occurred on higher stumps.

I made some notes, returned to my walking stick, set the new azimuth, and struck off for stand ⑥. Before too long I came to an extraction road that Johnny Cut-and-Run had bulldozed. What a mess! The roadbed hadn't been ditched or shaped. A dozer had simply grubbed (cleared the road of stumps) by pushing them to each side and that was the extent of the road "construction". Johnny had sold gravel from the pit to the Department of Transportation; none went on the woods road. Thus the "road" was now a muddy scar of deep, water-filled ruts that had recently been churned up by some mental midgets with room temperature I.Q.'s driving ATV's and 4 x 4's. I shook my head. ATV's and 4 x 4's are ok for some things…but "muddin'" certainly isn't one of them. Idiots!

I crossed the mud and continued through the hardwood clearcut until I reached stand ⑥. This stand hadn't been harvested. The overstory species consisted of about 40 foot (12 m) tall balsam fir, red spruce, red maple, yellow birch and scattered aspen. I bored* some trees and determined that the stand was even-aged and about 35 years old. It classified as a mixedwood stand* and I could see a few places that had a carpet of sphagnum moss which indicated areas of imperfect drainage. After making a few notes I set my azimuth and headed toward stand ⑦.

I had been interested in stand ⑦ since looking at it on the photo. The aerial photos were taken eight years ago and showed a very young regenerating stand. Eight years later here I was standing looking at a densely stocked softwood sapling stand. Leader* growth was from 6 to 10 inches (15-25 cm).

I paced to the center, hung a piece of flagging tape and wandered around in the stand. The trees looked healthy and vigorous. Species composition was balsam fir, red spruce, white birch, pin cherry and scattered red maple coppice. The average height was about 6 feet (1.8 m).

I cut off a balsam fir at ground level and aged it. It was advance regeneration.* This was easy to determine because of the ring pattern. Beginning at the pith I carefully counted five tightly spaced annual growth rings. From there to the bark the growth rings were more widely spaced. I then counted 9 years. This gave me two ages; the biological age of the fir which was 5 years plus 9 years equals 14 years; and the age since release* which was 9 years.

I thought about the age since release. Before the previous stand was harvested the advance fir and spruce had what are known as shade needles. Being shaded, they were less resistant to heat and moisture stress but could photosynthesize at low light conditions. When the previous stand was harvested, these needles had to physically adapt to higher light intensity by developing thicker cuticles and extra cells to make them more resistant to heat desiccation and water loss. This took time so, as a guess, I added a year to the age since release which the annual rings showed making it 10 years. Not a big deal, but fun to think through.

The stand was dense and I wanted to get a quick idea of the number of stems per hectare. To do this properly you must take a number of random samples scattered over the complete stand, but for my quick walk-through assessment I choose what I thought was a representative spot and did a stem count.

This is a simple procedure. I picked a tree for the center of my plot, and using my walking stick on which I had previously notched a 1.26 m mark, I swung a circle counting all the trees by species that were within the circumference of this circle. The count was 3 balsam fir, 2 red spruce, plus the center tree which was a white birch. This totals 6 trees. The trees per hectare factor for a 1.26 m radius is 2000, so 2000 times 6 equals 12 000 stems per hectare.

Other plot sizes can also be used. For example I often use either a 1.26 or 1.78 m radius before spacing* and a 3.99 m radius to check the stem count after the trees are spaced.

Here's a sample of plot radii and factors to determine stem density.

Plot size (ha)	Plot size (m²)	Plot radius (m)	Stems/ha factor
1/2000	5	1.26	2000
1/1000	10	1.78	1000
1/500	20	2.53	500
1/300	33.33	3.26	300
1/200	50	3.99	200

By tallying the trees by species I could easily calculate the tree species by percent.

Species	# Trees	Calculation	Percent species
Balsam fir	3	3/6 x 100	50
Red spruce	2	2/6 x 100	33
White birch	1	1/6 x 100	17
Total trees	6		100%

I like converting tree species numbers to percent because it gives me a sense of what can be done through management with a stand. In this case we have a stand that's about 33% spruce. This indicates to me that by favoring the spruce when spacing, thinning* and an eventual shelterwood* we have a good chance of encouraging a much higher percentage of spruce in the next rotation*.

It also tells me that since there's this much spruce there are more longer term management options for the stand because of the expected longevity of the spruce.

People sometimes ask me how to determine the number of trees per acre or hectare that would be there when using different spacing or planting widths. As long as you remember two numbers it's easy. If you're working in Imperial (inches, feet, acres) the number is 43,560 (the number of square feet in an acre). If you're working in metric (cm, m, ha) you must remember 10 000 (the number of square metres in a hectare).

For example: if trees are 6 feet apart, how many trees would be on an acre? You simply square 6 (6 ft. x 6 ft. = 36 ft.²) and divide the result into 43,560 (43,560 ft² = 1,210 trees per acre).
36 ft.²

Working in metric is similar. For example, how many trees are on a hectare at a spacing of 2 metres? Again square the distance (2 m x 2 m = 4 m²) and divide the result into 10 000

(10 000 m² = 2 500 trees per hectare).
4 m²

Perhaps you want to plant or space trees 2.4 metres apart? The calculations are the same (2.4 m x 2.4 m = 5.76 m²)

10 000 m² = 1 736 trees per hectare.
5.76 m²

As I wandered through the stand I also examined the old cut stumps. Some were probably about twelve-year old stumps, and were a good size and still reasonably sound, while other stumps were much more rotted. This led me to believe that a partial harvest or shelterwood* had been done in the past.

I knelt at a sound stump. It was about 18 inches (46 cm) in diameter, was spruce, and had been 78 years old when the tree was cut. Signs of annual ring release were still quite visible. By counting from the ring next to the bark in to where the rings were more crowded together I determined that the tree had been released about 15 years and before being cut. After release, the tree grew well for the next 15 years then was harvested. Since the regeneration's age since release was 10 years, this indicated that the more rotted stumps were 15 plus 10 or about 25 years old.

I looked at my watch. Two o'clock! I wrote some notes, changed the azimuth, and headed for stand ⑧ which was the old burn.

Stand ⑧ was composed of trembling aspen, gray birch, pin cherry, some scattered maple coppice, many snags, and lots of downed woody material. The average height ranged from 10 feet (3

m) to 13 feet (4 m) and the stand was densely stocked by vigorous hardwood root suckers, stump sprouts and some seed origin trees.

Curious as to when the area burned I aged one of the stems in a maple coppice. There were ten growth rings. Since the aerial photo I was using was taken eight years ago, it showed me what the area had looked like two years after the wildfire.

I looked around. The numerous stems in each of the coppice clumps and the relatively unharmed duff suggested that this had been a spring fire. At this time the parent maple in the coppice I had aged was killed by the fire, but since there was a lot of energy in its root system the adventitious* buds on the root collar had immediately sprouted, thus beginning regrowth the same year as the fire.

I sat on a large flat rock, pulled out my thermos, poured a cup of tea, and reflected on what I was seeing. When fighting wildfire or walking across quiet, fire blackened, still smouldering areas, that were once full of plant, bird, and wildlife, it's probably natural to think of fire as Nature's enemy. As utter destruction and waste.

But that's simply not true. Wildfire is natural and one of the main disturbances that Nature uses to periodically cleanse and renew itself. It's a successful process that's been recycling ecosystems for thousands of years.

I thought about the tree species here now and asked myself why they're here. The pin cherry was here because the heat from the then blackened post-fire landscape triggered germination in pin cherry seeds buried for as long as 150 years. The gray birch was probably here because of wind-blown seeds that landed on bare soil and, having no shade, germinated. However, the large tooth and trembling aspens are my favorite trees. Not because of their pretty or interesting grain pattern or figure; they're very plain and bland. Not because of their durability; they're not a very hard wood. And not because they, as a single tree, can live to an old age; they're a short-lived species living to about 100 years.

However, biologically and ecologically aspen is a unique and fascinating tree species. How many people know that it's the world's largest clone*? There's an aspen stand in Utah that covers 106 acres (43 ha) containing about 47,000 aspens that are genetically actually a single tree! It's not known how old this clone is, but it's assumed that a clone can date back to the last glaciation period which was about 10,000 years ago.

How many people realize that aspen bark is quite unique, that its outer layer is actually a phloem layer that can photosynthesis? That's why aspen bark has its characteristic greenish colour. This results in a highly nutritious browse* for bears, deer, snowshoe hares, porcupines, beaver, and many smaller mammals. Also, since there are male and female aspens, the male catkins (flower parts) are an important spring food source for ruffed grouse.

How many people consider the pH* of leaves and needles which carpet the forest floor? This appears to depend on the substrate* the tree was growing upon, but in general, softwood needles and hardwood leaves such as red oak are more acidic than aspen, ash, or elm leaves. The result is that aspen leaves tend to buffer forest soils thus making them a little less acidic... Nature's Tums or Rolaids?

Aspen can regenerate itself in three ways; by seed, stump sprout, and root sucker. Their seeds are light in weight and easily blown long distances on spring winds to recolonize disturbed areas. However, unlike some tree seeds, aspen seeds don't require stratification*. This means that they can germinate in the same year as they left the tree. In fact they have a short viability* of about two to three weeks.

Their ability to stump sprout is no big deal. Other hardwoods such as birch, beech, oak, maple, ash and pin cherry can do this as well. Other species can also root sucker, but it's the root suckering characteristics of aspen that fascinates me. Aspens have an extensive root system, often extending more than 100 feet (30 m) from the parent tree. Lateral roots* are undulating, rising and descending somewhat like a gentle ocean wave, while vertical sinker roots* near the tree firmly anchor it and help protect it from windthrow*. Located on the lateral roots are reproductive buds which can germinate when the ground is warmed by the sun. The buds near the surface of the forest floor usually germinate first but, if they happen to be killed by a surface fire, the buds on the bottom of the undulating root can still germinate because the deeper soil depth offers more protection from the heat of the fire. Thus they retain the ability to sucker.

As an aside, large tooth and trembling aspen roots can remain alive for a long time after the aspen is no longer visible in the canopy. These old, original aspen roots are sustained by short-term suckers that only survive for a few years in the shade; but they manage to keep the parent root alive. Interesting.

However, back to the wildfire. On a good site, a mature aspen root can generate 400,000 or more suckers per acre. These root suckers grow rapidly by extracting nutrients and water from the parent root system and can grow three to five feet (0.19 – 1.5 m) tall each year during the first few years. Thus, they are able to out compete other forest tree species. Aspen *must* win the height race, because it's shade intolerant,* which means that if it becomes shaded it eventually dies.

So how does this grossly overstocked stand survive? Simple. Aspen is self thinning* so a mature forest can, and usually will, develop from all of these suckers. But when you think about it, it's a bit of a paradox because these aspen clones will eventually need another disturbance such as a wildfire or clearcut in order to maintain themselves. Thus far they have maintained themselves very well, for aspen is the most widely distributed species in Canada. However, it's a species that is often considered to be only a weed species. Unfortunate.

My musings were interrupted when a big cow moose crashed out from the trees to my left. She stopped, looked around, but didn't notice me sitting there. After about a minute she lumbered away minding her own moose business. By the way, I knew it was a female moose because her long nose was brown in colour. Bull (male) moose have black noses.

I stood up and headed southerly through stand ⑤ until I came to one of Cut An' Run's extraction "roads" and followed its muddy scar back to my truck at the gravel pit. It had been a great day and I now felt that I was sufficiently acquainted with Roddie's new woodlot to be able to offer him some management options. But after having seen much of the lot, I couldn't agree with Roddie's description of it as being "skinned alive". Although some damaging and harmful harvesting practices had been inflicted on the woodlot there were still many management opportunities that we could and would explore. I smiled to myself. Roddie had whined that he had bought a "pig in a poke". Well, the "poke" might be a tad tattered, but at least the pig was still alive.

LETTERS, E-MAILS, PHONE CALLS, AND CONVERSATIONS

The job of teaching is to excite a boundless sense of curiosity about life, so that person shall apprehend it with an excitement tempered with awe and wonder.
- John Garrett

One aspect that I enjoy about my job is telling people the various ways that Nature functions. And it's good that I do enjoy it, because I'm often asked a wide variety of questions. Some I can answer immediately, but many force me to research the question before being able to get back to the person who requested information. Questions help me learn too. Let me give you some recent examples.

Last week I had a letter from one of the students in Mrs. Major's grade-three class. Here's how it read.

> Hi
> I am in grade 3 at the Big Spoon Cove School and I need to find out stuff about trees. My teacher tole me you know stuff about trees. I need to like know how the maple tree at our school loses its leaves in the autume.

Tell me a lot of stuff so I will get a 100.
Your friend
Billy Howe

I chuckled as I read Billy's letter and remembered the difficulties that I had with grammar and spelling when I was in grade 3. I turned to my computer and typed:

Dear Billy:

Thank you for asking me this interesting question. So that I can give you lots of stuff, I'll first tell you why maple trees lose their leaves and then tell you how it happens.

As you know we have very cold, windy winters here in Big Spoon Cove. Since leaves have a lot of water in them the cold would freeze this water and damage the leaves. So the tree avoids this by dropping its leaves in the autumn.

But before the tree drops its leaves the following things happen. First, there are some chemicals in the leaves such as nitrogen and phosphorus that the tree wants to keep and not lose when the leaf drops off, so the tree reabsorbs these elements so they can be used again the next year.

Next, there's a layer of cells where the leaf joins the branch. These cells begin to give off a chemical which weakens the leaf's hold on the branch and so the leaf eventually falls off.

Finally, cells form a protective layer over where the leaf was attached, just like a scrape on your knee heals over so you don't get infection from germs.

I hope this is some help to you and that you get 100 for your project.

And then of course there are e-mails. A few days after my presentation at the annual forestry meeting in New Harbour, I received the following e-mail from Jim Ferguson, a harvesting contractor from Little Spoon Cove.

I heard your speech at the forestry meeting and have these comments. As you know I am a harvesting contractor and have over a million and a half dollars owing on my machines. Therefore, I must keep them continually working in order to pay for the machines, fuel, maintenance, stumpage, employees and have something left for myself.

You said that we are cutting too much wood. If I don't cut the amount that I am cutting now (more would be better), myself and my employees are out of a job.

Are you saying that contractors should go the way of the dodo bird?

I would appreciate a reply. Knowing you I will get one. Knowing me, I might not like it.

After reading the e-mail I sat back and thought about Jim. I know both his and his crew's work. His company is one of the best, if not *the* best harvesting company in this area. Jim knows his stuff, is honest, and fair. I'd recommend him in a heartbeat.

I pushed 'reply' then typed:

Jim, I've known you for a long time and without any reservation say that you're a good contractor and I'd recommend you to anyone.

*I suggest that you missed the point of my talk. In one part of my speech I suggested that wood is being 'wasted' by the ever fattening weekend editions and flyers promoting retail stores. In my opinion, this wood should be better used for longer-lasting things rather than fat newspapers. We **need** wood and we need knowledgeable people to harvest it. Again, in my opinion, you'll not be, to use your phrase, 'going the way of the dodo bird'.*

Having said that, I wouldn't mind seeing the 'cut and run' gang join the dodos tomorrow. There's no place in sustainable forestry for this careless, unethical crowd.

If I haven't addressed your concerns, please give me a call and let's discuss them over a coffee at Mings.

Telephones are also a part of my day. Because I work in forestry some of the public think I know the hunting, fishing, trapping, or camping park regulations. I don't. When I try to direct their question to someone who can help them, it seems that an increasing number of callers are now rather rude, some are even offensive. Perhaps it's a sign of the times. I hope not.

But then there are the interesting calls. Like the one I received two weeks ago from Eugene MacLennan who owns a small woodlot near New Harbour. Gene said he was calling on behalf of a group of himself and five others who wanted to learn how to grow shiitake mushrooms.

Shiitake mushrooms? Interesting. I told Gene that I didn't know anything about growing them but knew a mycologist who might be able to help. I said that I'd get back to him.

After I hung up the phone I called Genna Kennedy. Genna and her husband Peter live over on West Mountain and have a seasonally diverse business called Nature's Gifts. They sell honey, mushrooms, fuelwood, maple syrup, and Christmas trees; rhubarb, herbs and garlic from their large organic garden; and trout from their pond.

Peter and Genna are an interesting couple. Peter, a civil engineer, and Genna, who has a Master's degree in mycology, had both come to hate their jobs in Ontario. The couple finally decided to do something about it, so they quit their jobs and moved back home to West Mountain. They bought an abandoned farm, and by working from dawn to dusk were now happily living their shared dreams.

I phoned Genna and luckily caught her in the house. After small talk about weather, crops, and markets, I asked her if she would be interested in teaching a half-day course to Gene and his group on how to grow shiitakes.

"I'd love to," she replied. "We've been growing them here for the past five years and I've learned a lot about them, unfortunately mainly through trial and error. Let's do it on a Saturday and as soon as possible, because before too long I'll be too busy here and won't be able to go."

I told Genna that I had access to a small training budget, so we agreed on an honorarium for her travel and four-hour course, then set a tentative date. Simple as that.

The course was to be held on the last Saturday of the month. As news spread, eight people signed up for Genna's course.

She called me on the Tuesday before the course and gave me a list of materials needed to teach her eight candidates. I wrote:

8 pieces of hardwood 4 to 8 inches (10-20 cm) in diameter, 3 to 4 feet (1-1.2 m) long. Genna suggested sugar maple or white ash and cautioned against using red oak or pine logs because of their fungicidal chemicals.

4 electric drills with 5/16" wood-boring bits for dowel spawn logs (3/8" bits for sawdust spawn).

4 hammers.

Food-grade wax and a package of sponge wax daubers.

Genna said she would supply the dowel spawn and also had some handout material which she asked if I would photocopy on the Saturday morning of the class.

Saturday finally came, and so did the rain! We met at the Department of Natural Resources depot workshop in Little Spoon Cove. Since I thought that I would also try my hand at growing shiitakes, I kept notes and although they're in point form I've reproduced them here for the reader.

SHIITAKE MUSHROOMS – PRESENTER GENNA KENNEDY.

Course candidates: Eugene MacLennan, Ann Sampson, Roddie McInnis, Mike Stanley, Gladys Richards, Bob Adams, 'Red' Angus MacAllister, and John 'Pecker' Robinson.

- Third most widely produced mushroom in the world.
- Medicinal benefits: anti-tumour and antiviral effects, reduce high blood pressure, lower cholesterol, contain vitamins A, B, B12, C, D, Niacin, good source of protein.
- Typically produced under forest shade. Mixedwood stands best (hardwoods provide extra shade in summer).
- Situate near good water source i.e., pond/brook.
- Logs for inoculation: white oak (best), elm, beech, hard maple, white ash and yellow birch.
- Logs: cut when dormant (4-8" diameter [10-2cm]/3-4' [1-1.2 m] long).
- Logs: inoculate within two weeks after cutting to prevent infection from other fungi.
- Spawn: may either purchase dowel plugs or sawdust blocks. Important – use best strain of spawn for your area.
- Inoculation: drill a row of holes about 1 to 1 ½" (2.5 to 3.8 cm) deep, 6 inches (15 cm) apart along the length of the log. Next, roll the log about 2 inches (5 cm) and drill another

row of holes locating each hole on this line of holes midway between the holes on the first row. Continue turning the log about 2 inches (5 cm) and drilling a row of holes until you have rows of holes around the circumference of the log.

Everyone teamed up with a partner and the sound of drills filled the shop.

At 10' o'clock we stopped for coffee or tea, Ming's huge ham and cheese biscuits, Peter's honey, and Genna's wine jelly. The questions started. I sat back and took notes.

Through a mouthful of honey-laced biscuit Mike asked Genna how many logs it would take for a little shiitake business.

"It depends on how big you want to grow your business," replied Genna. "We have about 5,000 logs but we're really a small-scale operation. For your own use you might only want to have a dozen or two logs. As I said, it depends."

Ann Sampson asked Genna if there were any risks.

"Yes, there certainly are. Your biggest problem will likely be moisture during the summer. Long hot, dry spells reduce mushroom quality and yield. That's why I suggest you keep your logs next to a clean reliable brook or pond. And then of course there are slugs, mice, squirrels, birds, and deer to contend with. It can get interesting."

"How do you know how much spawn to buy?" asked Gene.

"It's a bit of a guess," replied Genna. "Assuming 35 to 40 holes per log you're looking at about a $1000 to $1200 worth of spawn to inoculate 1000 logs. This is using dowel-type spawn. The sawdust type will probably cost you about $600 to $800 to inoculate the same number of logs."

"Genna," asked Gladys, "How soon after inoculation will there be shiitakes?"

"Well Gladys, you'll know that fruiting will soon follow when you see the fungal white mycelia* on the ends of your logs. But how long? It again depends on the number of things. But let's say between six to eighteen months after they're inoculated."

Genna turned to the group. "Well folks, what say we get back to work?

"Just one more question Genna," said Pecker. "How long will the inoculated log keep producing?"

"That depends on the log diameter John," replied Genna. "As long as things go well, about three to five years. Incidentally, Peter and I have found that the second and third year's crops are nearly twice as large as the first year's crop. Ok," she said. "Let's inoculate these logs."

Genna demonstrated by hammering the little plugs of spawn into the holes. Then, using a sponge, she applied a thin coating of hot wax over the spawn-filled holes to prevent other fungal spores from gaining entrance to the logs.

When the group had filled and waxed their logs Genna said, "Now that our logs are prepared, we have to stack them in a shaded place. Peter and I stack ours in the woods near our fish pond.

"There are two ways to stack them, either log-cabin style or lean-to style. You must remember two important things. First, you need good air circulation around your logs to prevent molds from growing, and second, you must never let the inside of your logs dry out. During spawn incubation, Peter and I water our logs using a pump and sprinkler system and water them for about 12 hours once or twice a month depending on the weather. If you have just a dozen or two logs for family use you could immerse them in an old bathtub filled with water."

"What 'bout harvestin' 'em?" asked Roddie.

"We harvest when the mushroom caps are about two-thirds open. Just cut the mushroom stem flush with the bark using a sharp knife. Keep the shittakes in a cardboard box in a cool place."

The talk slowly changed from mushroom growing to village gossip and the class ended. I thanked Genna for her excellent presentation, her shiitake spawn, jelly, and Peter's honey, and was just about to turn and mingle with the group when Roddie spoke up.

"Jist a minute! My wife an' former sweetheart Jean iss takin' bowl turnin' lessons from Matthew, an' she wants ta give ya a spalted bowl thet she made. I ain't much fer speeches, but you an' Peter hev done a lotta good work on yer farm an' are always willin' ta share yer knowledge. So here!"

Everyone nodded and clapped while a red-faced Genna accepted the bowl.

Later, after everyone left, and while Roddie and I were sweeping, Roddie said, "Ya know, there's still awful good people 'round here. Help ya in the wink of an eye. But yerself! Ya neffer did tell me how old thet spruce wass thet ya cut thet day at the bog."

I had sanded and aged the cut section of the tree but had indeed forgotten to tell Roddie until I was reminded when I saw his name on the list for Genna's course. I now had it in my pocket and passed it to him. On the side I had marked its age.

"A hundred an' eleven years! Holy jumpin' wait 'till I tells Jin Alek. By the way, when are ya goin' ta take a walk over me new woodlot?"

I told Roddie that I had done so last week and had an idea that I'd like him to consider. We sat for about a half an hour while I outlined my plan. Roddie sat back, rubbed his pipe on the side of his nose and finally said, "Let's do it. Git back ta me if ya needs any help. Ya know, fer someone from away yer not *all* thet bad. Maybe in 10 er 15 years Jean'll think thet yer fit ta give a bowl ta too."

I took it as a compliment and smiled.

BARBEQUES, BANTER, AND BELIEFS

Appreciation of the vast complexity of forest ecosystems means confronting the limitations of our knowledge. This will require both learning to cope with uncertainties so that we are not paralyzed to act, and adopting a sense of humility in forest endeavours.
—Kathryn Kohm and Jerry Franklin

Following the shiitake workshop, Roddie was excited by my suggestion about discussing the management of his new woodlot. It was a simple idea. He would come up with a list of his objectives for the lot; I in turn, would invite some of my forestry colleagues to a barbeque next Saturday at Roddie's camp. I would bring the steaks, Roddie said Jean would provide the salad. The purpose of the barbeque was two fold. To have a pleasant afternoon with friends, and to discuss some ideas about ecological restoration.

Soon after I got to the office that Monday morning Stanley Farquar phoned. Stanley, a retired banker, had built a rental cottage on his woodlot that was now becoming widely known as an ideal get-away-from-it-all lodging. He told me it was now rented for a month to an author from Carlsbad, California. Stanley said the woman was just finishing her manuscript called Nature: Our Teacher – How To Reawaken Your Connection. He told me that her name was Ann Warnica, Ph.D, and thought that I should meet her.

Later that day I had to go out Stanley's way to check on a spacing that one of the silviculture contractors was doing on Hector MacDonald's woodlot, so I dropped in to see Stanley and Doris.

My rap on the screen door was answered by Stanley's, "Come on in and have a cup of tea!"

Stanley, his wife Doris, and a woman I didn't know sat around the kitchen table. I was quickly introduced to the stranger. Ann Warnica smiled and stood up to shake hands. She was a tall woman with long, dark brown hair, a pleasant smile, blue eyes, and the deepest female voice I had ever heard; she actually sounded like she gargled with sand. And what a knuckle crunching grip!

I sat and had a cup of tea with them and during the course of our small talk invited them all to the barbeque at Roddie's camp the next Saturday. After consulting Doris, the dog, the kitchen calendar, yellow sticky notes, his pocket calendar, blackberry, the newspaper's weekly astrological forecast and probably running it by Nostradamus, Stanley said it looked like perhaps he could attend after all. In case you didn't know, Stanley was an obsessive compulsive banker with a bad facial twitch when he retired to Big Spoon Cove. At least the twitch was gone now anyway. Doris and Ann readily agreed to come. Doris said she would bring a rhubarb upside-down cake, Ann volunteered a bottle of single-malt scotch. Not be outdone, Stanley said he would bring Doris and Ann. What a guy!

It started to rain heavily Friday night, but by Saturday it got down to serious raining. I had never seen it rain harder as I backed my truck up to the deck at Roddie's camp. It was good that he had roofed it over. We could barbeque on the deck. However, it was raining so hard that when I stepped under the tin roof it sounded like I was inside a snare drum played by an exuberant four-armed drummer on speed. Or at least strong coffee!

I mouthed a "hello" to Roddie. We unloaded the cooler of steaks, the two barbeques, and went in and closed the door. Ahh... quieter.

I wiped the rain off my glasses and looked around. There was Roddie, his wife Jean, Frugal, Brother Thomas, Doris, Stanley, Ann Warnica, and Fred King. Fred is an ecology professor over at the University of Environmental Science in New Harbour. He's a short, portly man sporting a lattice-effect comb over; perfectly-round aluminum-bound glasses perched on a little perfectly-round red, boozer's nose that has more busted veins than the Klondike, below which hangs an untrimmed salt and pepper beard nearly down to his western belt buckle. Fred's complete name is Frederick Urban King, which is perhaps unfortunate for a demanding professor, because his students refer to him as "The F U King." I also heard the comment from a student that old FU talks so slow that you could walk between the words, and also that his mouth is so slanted that he has to talk in *Italics*. However, Fred is an extremely intelligent man, and a good friend. Roddie once remarked that Fred had more letters after his name than you could find in a bowl of Campbell's alphabet soup.

As I sat in one of the rocking chairs there was a loud stamping on the deck, and amid the jingle of bottles, in came John Alex wearing a raincoat large enough to shelter three close friends. He carried a case of Keith's ale.

"Ah, Jin Alek," cried Roddie. "I could hear them Cape Breton wind chimes all the way from yer truck. Put yer beer by the sink an' pull up a chair."

Roddie looked around an winked. "Jin Alek didn't think he'd make it taday. Gut a big renovatin' job ta do ta hiss privy." He looked over at me. "Ya knows, the leanin' one thet's held tagether by cobwebs an' where ole flies goess ta die. Goin' ta reshingle it.

Tole me thet ya neffer know when company might drop by."

Ann looked horrified and probably wondered what she had gotten into by coming here.

John Alex smiled and said, "Telephone, telegraph er tell Roddie. A penny saved iss still jist a penny, eh?" With those words of wisdom John Alex subsided into a chair.

Everyone settled back in their chairs and looked expectantly at Roddie. He looked around, "What are ya starin' at me fer? It's the young fella over there thet called this meetin'!" All eyes then turned to me.

I smiled. "Since we have some new people in our little fire-side group and the topic of our get together is forest restoration, let's begin by introducing ourselves and perhaps sharing our personal philosophy or feelings on forests, woodlots, Nature…your choice."

"I'll begin," said Ann. "My name is Ann Warnica and I'm presently writing a book on the social impact of our ever increasing alienation from the natural world. With increasing human urbanization there's becoming a serious disconnect with the natural world. In my book, I quote William Ruckelshaus who said, 'The Earth is real, and we are obliged by the fact of our utter dependence on it, to listen more closely to its messages'. It's difficult to *listen more closely to it's messages* if you're living in an asphalt jungle, especially in our crime infested inner cities. I believe that this ever-increasing disconnect is one of the root causes for the crime, drug, and hopelessness experienced by our youth. In my book I explore ways to enhance our social well-being by reconnecting with Nature. That's where I'm coming from."

"Let me go next, I'm Dr. Jean MacInnis, Roddie's favourite first wife and former sweetheart. I'm a forester working with Natural Resources Canada on a number of projects, two of them being carbon sequestration and climate change. I guess I view Nature as an intricate perpetual-motion machine. However, it's a machine that humans have and are damaging by our over population, over exploitation, and wasteful lifestyles. Who wants to go next?"

"Hi, ahh, I'm Flewellen MacDougall, better known as Frugal. I'm a wildlife biologist, so naturally my main interest is wildlife, their habits and habitat. I'm deeply concerned about habitat destruction caused by the over use of clearcutting, by deforestation,[*] by wetland reduction, by fragmentation[*]...I could go on, but let's just say that in general I'm deeply concerned about the welfare and indeed the survival of fish, birds and wild animals. Next?"

"I'm John Alex MacDonald, eh? I hev a woodlot thet I used ta harvest. Gettin' a tad long in the tooth fer thet now, so's I only uses me lot fer firewood ta keep me an' Martha warm; fer a few logs if'n I needs some lumber; and I cuts enough pulpwood every year ta pay me taxes. Gut some nice stands a spruce thet I really don't want ta cut, eh? The money from them 'll bury me an' Martha. We're all in thiss tagether by ourselves, eh? Who's next?"

"Ahh, yes, let me see, I'm Fred King, professor of ecology over at UES in New Harbour. When I was young I had an old, rather eccentric uncle who lived alone in a little cabin in the woods. I used to spend any time I could with him because together we would explore ant hills, rotten logs, rock piles, swamps, whatever. As a result, or perhaps it's genetic, I developed an insatiable thirst to learn about and try to understand the wonderous world of natural cycles and the interconnectedness of every microorganism, insect, bird, fish, mammal, and even humans. Ahh, I've since learned that everything is connected to everything else, so that in fact we are one giant organism consisting of many interdependent little parts. A humbling realization, to say the least. What do you think Tom?"

"Well, I'm Brother Thomas, a Trappist hermit who lives much like Fred's old uncle, for I also live in a little cabin in the woods and, when I think about it, perhaps I too am eccentric. At least my little pug probably often thinks so. To me Nature, whether it be a forest, lake, stream, or even desert is a place where I experience a spiritual renewal. I really can't tell you why. It just feels to me that

I'm amid an on-going magical creation; that life comes from death and without death there could be no renewal of life. And of course Nature enhances my meditation and contemplation not only on the creation, but also on the Creator. I often tell people that I study both the book of God's word and the book of God's works. What do you think Doris?"

"Hi, I'm Doris Farquar, Stanley's wife. Perhaps I don't have such a spiritual connection to Nature, but I do appreciate and even need its beauty. A painted trillium, snow clinging to trees, sunsets, geese honking as they pass overhead; or even to lie on my back in the new spring grass and watch the clouds. Sounds silly I guess, but it's important to me anyway. Isn't that right dear?"

"Yes," said Stanley. "I'm her husband, Stanley, and I can attest to the fact that Doris needs and sees beauty in Nature. You might not know it, but Doris is a graduate of the Nova Scotia College of Art and Design. She's an artist and sells her paintings through an art dealer in Vancouver. As for me, a retired banker, I'm interested in Nature from an eco-tourism point of view. That's why I had the retreat cabin built and that's why I'm having two more built this summer. In this fast-paced, changing world, there's a good dollar to be made by sharing my woodlot with the frazzled crowd that I used to run with back in the city. And you know, it's a simple, but healthy lifestyle too here in Big Spoon Cove. I'm feeling much better physically and mentally now that I'm living this rural lifestyle."

Doris looked over to me. "So, we all know you, but I for one would like to hear what your thoughts are on Nature. Let's hear them."

I had been listening carefully and was amazed at the diversity of opinions from our small group. Everything from social, spiritual, wildlife, aesthetic and economic values; to global climate concerns, and even basic scientific curiosity. Quite a range indeed.

I scratched my head. "The short answer is that I'm fascinated by the wows, hows, and whys of Nature; but I'll be more specific. In my view, Nature shouldn't be considered as a 'resource', because to me this implies something that's there to be exploited for human wants and needs. Humans are but one of all the species that occupy this solitary planet spinning through space.

"Every living thing must share the Earth's air, water, and bounty from a fragile soil or sea that covers this spaceship. Many things which the Earth provides are finite and not inexhaustible. But as humans, we *need* things such as wood, minerals, oil, etc. that only Nature can supply. So we must balance our economic stability with environmental sustainability. Think about it. Nature has a mechanism called disturbance[*] which has been effectively renewing and adjusting the evolution of this planet for millions of years; decreasing what is too much, and increasing what is too little. This tells me that we too much strive for a balance. That it's imperative that we use a more ecological approach. Forest managers and the general public must take a hard look at their attitudes and values toward Nature. Being human, what we don't understand and respect...we often tend to use and abuse. I believe that greater understanding and respect will result in an improved stewardship of the lands and oceans.

"Notice I said 'improved' stewardship. Many present forest management decisions are based on outdated information. We've learned a lot about the workings of Nature during the last two decades. We now *know* that many old forest management techniques simply aren't sustainable over a number of stand rotations. But they're still being used, and even touted as being sustainable and good stewardship by those who should know better. However, sustainability of Nature's systems and processes will only be achieved by long-term ecological management, and not, as in many cases today, by short-term economic concerns.

"Think about it this way. 'Ecology' is the house; 'economy' is the management of the house. With improper and short-sighted economic mismanagement, the house soon slips further into disrepair...until it eventually collapses. Sorry, I'll get down from my soapbox now."

"Yiss, yiss", said Roddie. "Ass I offen tells Jin Alek, ask thiss guy fer the time an' he starts by tellin' ya how ta build a watch. But I agrees with what yer sayin', even though I think ya wass vaccinated by a gramophone needle.

"Ya said *respect* fer Nature. I 'member me ole man sayin' thet there ain't any *away* when ya throws things away.

"I'm goin' ta be a tad shorter in my thoughts 'bout Nature. Ta me the woodlot gives me three things. First, it's money standin' on the stump. Ya kin always send a load a studwood er logs over ta Northport Lumber. Second, I spends a lot a time here alone at the camp er in the woods...I jist likes it. And third, when I puts on the wings an' white nightie an' gits inta the pine canoe the woodlots will go ta the kids. Land iss gettin' more expensive effery year, an' by the time they're growed maybe they won't be able ta afford ta buy any fer themselves.

"Now, we're here ta hev a feed an' talk 'bout me new woodlot. But first, I wants efferyone ta try a small libation of what I called *Roddie's Elixir-A Fine Wart An' Hemorrhoid Remover.*" He went over to the cupboard, took out glasses and a bottle of yellowish liquid containing tiny green and red peppers and poured everyone a small drink.

After the traditional *'Cheers'*, we all downed the drink. Eyes teared. Necks and ears got red. Nothing was said. Fred's lattice hair stood up like a field of dandelions gone to seed. Suddenly Brother Thomas croaked, "The red roaring flames' of hell are rolling through my stomach! This jeesless stuff would make a saint swear! Get me some water John Alex."

"I can't," cried John Alex, who looked like he just swallowed James Brown, "Me asteroids are welded ta the chair!"

It was indeed a muscular drink, but soon everyone was laughing and comparing stories about its awesome effects. Perhaps Stanley summed it up best when he remarked that it might just be a figment of his intoxication, but Doris had bought him a pair of Stanfield's Fruit Of The Looms and he thought that now both the fruit and the looms were just a charred memento of *Roddie's Elixir – A Fine Scorcher of Men's Nether Garments.*"

"Yiss, yiss, slick ass a new blade shave", said Roddie. "Good stuff! If'n I could jist give me woodlot a good swig of thet Elixir it would be healthy in no time flat, what?"

An interesting thought. I turned and asked Fred what was his description of a healthy forest.

"Ahh, yes, let me see. A healthy forest you ask? A healthy forest has attained a balance between life and death. There are things constantly dying such as leaves, needles, plants, trees, herbivores,[*] fungivores[*] and predators.[*] When a forest is balanced this death nourishes life. It's like Brother Thomas said, 'Death and killing are essential for life to exist'.

"But, ahh, here's the thing you must understand. In order to attain this healthy balance there must be biological diversity.[*] In short, there must be enough parts in the system to allow the whole to work efficiently. It's like a car engine, remove a spark plug and the vehicle will limp along although it will operate inefficiently. Remove another part and the thing won't go at all. Aldo Leopold said it best, 'To keep every cog and wheel is the first precaution of intelligent tinkering'. We are, in fact, 'tinkering' with Nature.

"I agree," I said. "However, don't many of our forest management techniques tend to simplify a forest and lessen biodiversity? I'm thinking of a species-simple, short-rotation plantation. Also, we may truncate,[*] both ends of a rotation – first by herbicides which kill vegetation which humans don't want, and then by harvesting trees when they reach an economical size rather than allowing them to live to an older, biodiversity-friendlier age.

"So, in my view, through management we've lost some biodiversity in order to produce wood quicker. Is this loss harmful?"

"I don't think that it is in the short term," replied Jean. "The Acadian forest is very resilient.* I do however, have serious reservations about some of the management techniques of many industrial forests. In my view, this corporate, profit-driven approach will degrade potential forest productivity over a number of rotations."

"Not only degrading fibre productivity," said Frugal. "They've certainly degraded old growth habitat; have buggered up the habitat for early and late successional wildlife and bird species; and then there's water siltation an fragmentation!"

It wasn't often that Frugal got angry, but he was working up to it now and his frustrations were starting to surface. Time to fire up the barbeques.

The salad, steak, and rhubarb upside down cake were all delicious. During the meal, John Alex suddenly said, "Did ya know thet when I wass young me ole man usta make me stand in the hall closset? Said thet it wass elevator practice. I usta stand there fer hours. Martha said thet wass why, when she researched our MacDonald family tree, she discovered thet I'm the sap, eh."

After we finished a small dram of Ann's Scotch she said, "I'm a person who must see the whole picture before I concentrate on the details. What does Roddie's new woodlot look like?"

I described the different stands in detail. When I had finished Jean smiled. "Good description. I took a walk over the lot last week. She winked at me. I didn't want Roddie trailing along asking questions either. So we have a 20-acre old field softwood clearcut, a

30-acre hardwood clearcut with all tops and slash removed This adds up to 50 acres that have been cut. There's also 18 acres in the bog, pond and gravel pit. This leaves a 15-acre mixedwood stand, a 10-acre softwood sapling* stand and the naturally regenerating 7-acre old burn.

"Fred, she asked, "Do you have any broad, general ecological guidelines that should serve as a goal for what you would consider a healthy forest?"

"Ahh, yes, let me see," replied Fred as he laced his fingers across his belly. "Ecological guidelines you ask? Let me simply list what comes to mind. Renew the biological landscape by adding, protecting, or encouraging biological diversity; harvest trees at an older age rather than whenever they're big enough; make sure forests are interconnected; integrate plant pathogens and mycorrhizae* into our management techniques; use alternative silvicultural * approaches to harvesting; manage at the stand* level but integrate this into the shifting mosaic* of the landscape level; and finally, educate both the forest managers and the public in what should be done and why."

Fred then looked around at us through his perfectly round glasses. "Well, any questions class?"

It was John Alex that spoke. "Fred, ya keeps sayin' 'biodiversity'. Kin ya explain jist what ya means?"

"Ahh yes, yes, let me see now. When I say biodiversity I'm actually referring to five levels. First there's genetic diversity which means a genetic variation within a species. Then there's species diversity which refers to the variety of species in an area. Next, we have ecosystem* diversity, which means a variety of communities* or ecosystems in an area. The fourth is landscape diversity, which is the variety of ecosystems across a landscape. And finally, we have regional diversity, which refers to the variety of species, communities, ecosystems, or landscapes within a specific geographic region.

"Now, there's something else which I must point out. Yes, yes, I must point this out. There are three components of biodiversity in each level. There's compositional diversity. This includes such things as the number of species, genes, communities or ecosystems. Then there's structural diversity. By this I mean habitat structure, population structure, and the form, or in other words, the 'architecture' of structure. The third component is functional diversity, which looks at the number of ecological processes such as disturbance regimes,* what species do in a community, and the cycling of nutrients. Is that clear?"

"Yiss, yiss," replied Roddie. "Probably ta a nuclear physicist sech ass Jin Alek. Fred, I wass kind a lookin' fer more practical ideas." He looked at me. "Listenin' ta *him* iss like starin' at a cow fer an hour. What doess you haff ta say young fella?"

"Well," I replied, "Our understanding of Nature's complex interactions and interdependencies is still in its infancy. We know that we must do something, so we should proceed with caution if we're going to attempt to 'help' Nature's dynamics. But first, in my view, there are three things that *must* be understood before undertaking any woodlot management or forest restoration. First, you don't have to treat every acre or hectare. Second, you can't do everything on a 100 acre woodlot. And third, sometimes no treatment is the best thing to do.

"We can discuss silvicultural treatment options and wildife habitat considerations later. For now, let's just discuss the ecological end of management. In my view, there are nine areas to consider. In no particular ranking, these are longer rotations; selection management* when possible; the protection of soils; the retention of legacy trees; the retention and protection of snags and dead wood; the protection of keystone* species; the on-going maintenance of a carefully designed road system; the enhancement of biodiversity; and protection of all water sources and courses.

"I agree with your nine areas to consider," said Jean. "But if I were to rank one as being the most important I would have to choose the protection of soils. Without this thin layer that nourishes life the ball game is over…forever as far as the human species is concerned.

"So, how kin we protect soil me little voluptuous vamp?" asked Roddie.

Jean laughed and said to Ann, "You must understand that my husband's mind is similar to an inner-city railway; straight to the point, one track…and dirty. But he's something like a wart, I got used to him. However, to answer the question, soils must be protected from wind and water erosion by maintaining vegetative cover; from excessive compaction by using brush mats to support harvesting equipment; by using designated extraction trails rather than driving all over the area; or by reducing our tendency to construct too many access roads that are in many cases also much wider than necessary.

"However Roddie, my main concern is soil degradation which is mainly brought about by some of our so-called management practices. These include the removal of slash from the harvested site. Elements * such as nitrogen, potassium, and magnesium are mainly in the foliage while calcium is contained in the bark. By taking these valuable elements off site, long-term productivity is reduced.

"Another example of improper management that has an effect on soil is shorter rotations. Site productivity is reduced because of elements lost to the site that are contained in the wood removed. The ratio of sapwood to heartwood is higher in younger stands. This sapwood has higher mineral element concentrations than heartwood. So, shortening the rotation increases the proportion of sapwood vs. heartwood thus leading to loss of valuable elements from the site."

"Ah, yes, let me see," nodded Fred. "I agree with Jean, but let's also look at his point on the enhancement of biodiversity. Ahh yes, how do you suggest that we do it?"

I scratched my head. "Well, let's start at the beginning."

"We knowed this wass comin', eh Jin Alek?"

I grinned and continued. "The biological diversity of an area is dynamic; insects, birds, wildlife, and plant and tree species change through time. Think about secondary succession *. Over a period of time we move from a site, say disturbed by fire, to it being occupied by herbaceous vegetation, then shrubs, then shade intolerant species, then shade tolerant species and finally climax or old-growth species. Over this time line of changing vegetation species, bird and mammal species have also changed from those that require open conditions to those that require old forests. Speaking about old forests, about 25% of all wildlife species require large old trees or snags. And so, in my view we can encourage more biodiversity with woodlot or landscape level management by having an array of successional seres * and also by not eliminating the complex early and late ends of succession."

"What do you mean, early and late?" asked Ann.

"Early succession are the herbaceous, shrub and shade intolerant states. This is also known as the pioneer stage where often many different plant and tree species invade disturbed areas in large numbers, and where certain species seem to promote the establishment of other future species.

"Late succession refers to old-growth forests which usually contain large old trees, large snags, downed logs and a patchy understory. However, these forests can vary in tree size, age classes, structural elements, and understory* presence or absence."

"Yiss, yiss," cried Roddie, "I sees, early succession would be like Mrs. Major's grade three class. Late succession would be like ole Mrs. Major herself, what!"

"Roddie!" said Jean.

Ann turned to Fred. "What are legacy trees?"

"Ahh yes, yes, legacy trees you ask. Ahh, legacy trees or leave trees are trees that are designated to be left standing usually in small groups in the riparian zone or at the edge of harvested areas for cross pollination* reasons, for seed production, and wildlife so as to provide a biological legacy to the site following the harvest. Now, ahh, yes, by the term biological legacy, I mean an organism or biologically derived structure left from a previous ecosystem. This includes old trees, snags, and downed logs as these biologically and structurally enrich the new forest. Ahh, yes, is that clear my dear?"

Ann looked at him with a blank expression.

Frugal said, "Another way to look at it Ann is to put it into human terms. We write wills which are meant to insure that things are passed on to the next generation after we die. Well, Nature doesn't write a will, but does leave such things as long buried viable seeds; serotinous* or semi-serotinous cones such as jack pine cones which require heat to open before the seed can be released; the ability of killed trees to regenerate asexually from buds on the root collar or roots; Nature can also leave soil organisms such as bacteria, fungi, invertebrates etc., that can also help establish a few forest following a disturbance such as a wildfire, ice storm, hurricane, clearcut etc."

Frugal looked over at me, "I suggest that you change your term legacy trees into the more general term, biological legacy."

As I nodded my agreement Doris said, "I hear you guys saying that Nature is healthy and functioning properly when there's a landscape messed up by dead standing trees, probably all full of woodpecker holes, and with dead logs and limbs strewn all about. That's not my long-held idea of a neat, inviting forest. And certainly not the mess that I find beautiful and wish to paint. I'm confused."

Ann sat ahead in her chair. "Doris, try letting Nature be your teacher. Open yourself not only to the vista of landscapes, but also to the beauty and mastery of what I call eyescapes. Things like the fragile beauty of a painted trillium, a luna moth, a house fly's wing. Things like the sun on a dew-filled spider web, a heavy layer of green moss growing on a rotting log, or a single dandelion seed. But if Nature *is* to be your teacher you must be prepared to carefully observe and listen so you can understand her teachings."

"I totally agree Ann," said Brother Thomas. "Nature has always been an inspirational touchstone for both artists and would-be saints. Reminds me of that short poem by William Blake: *To see the world in a grain of sand, / and a heaven in a wildflower;/hold infinity in the palm of your hand,/ and eternity in an hour.*"

"Yiss, yiss, I'd drink ta thet if'n Jin Alek wass ta open thet case a beer."

"Go get it yerself. Jist because ya gut a crack in yer arse don't make ya a cripple, eh?"

"Well, as an artist I still call it a mess," said Doris, she hesitated then smiled. "Perhaps it's simply abstract or modern art. I'm a traditionalist I guess."

When John Alex was passing around the beer, he looked at me and asked, "What's a keystone, eh?"

As I unscrewed the beer cap I replied, "A keystone is something in Nature, be it a species, a habitat, or something else, that does something that a large part of the rest of the community depends upon. I'm thinking of carnivores * such as a fox that controls the population of herbivores such as mice or snowshoe hares. Then herbivores such as moose and white-tail deer can either promote diversity by preventing one or a few plant species from dominating a site, or on the other hand, they can reduce plant diversity by feeding on certain plants. Some plants themselves affect a larger community. Think of legumes or alders which add nitrogen to the soil, or cedars and maples which accumulate calcium.

"Ahh, yes, yes," said Fred. "But don't forget the bees. For without their pollinating and cross pollinating, the plants wouldn't be able to produce seeds for reproduction, and indeed for fruits, vegetables and grains. Many people don't realize that over 30% of the food we eat is bee-pollinated. And ahh, yes, then there's nitrogen-fixing bacteria and mycorrhizal fungi to consider too."

"That's very true," I replied. "Next, there are builders such as beavers that provide habitats for other species of insects, fish, birds and mammals."

"What!" said Stanley. "Beavers? They flood areas and kill trees. How can you possibly suggest that they're important enough to be a keystone? They're not builders, they're destroyers!"

"Well, I'm afraid you've fallen into the common trap of assigning human values to Nature's processes," I replied. "These values tell you that dead trees are a waste of wood and thus money. Both the terms 'waste' and the concept of 'money' are human inventions. Neither exist in Nature. Anyhow, back to the beaver. As you know, they build dams which hold a shallow pond that provides perhaps several acres of ecosystem for aquatic insects, flying insects, frogs, turtles, fish, ducks, geese, muskrats, mink, and even vegetation for large mammals such as moose.

"Another keystone is dead trees and downed logs. At one time, anything that was dead wasn't thought of as being a keystone, but when you consider that snags provide homes for cavity-nesting birds and many insect species; that downed logs provide a rich habitat for fungi, lichens, mosses, microbes, invertebrates, some small mammals; and how the decaying wood enriches the soil by providing a slow release of nitrogen and other elements, you realize what an important role they play in ecosystem function and process. Without them, sites are degraded in flora* and fauna* richness and also in fertility."

"Don't you think the term 'dead' wood is misleading?" asked Jean. "There's far more life in 'dead' wood than in 'living' wood. In the bole of a living tree there are about 5% living cells by volume, whereas in a dead one there can be up to 40%, primarily consisting of fungi and nitrogen-fixing bacteria.

"Ahh, yess, yess," nodded Fred. "But you see my dear, you must remember that all the *wood* in a tree is biologically dead tissue. Ahh, yes, dead. Just think about it. Wood is made up lignin-strengthened cellulose cell walls after the living material in the cell is removed. That being the case, the only living part of a tree's trunk and limbs is the cell layer that's under the bark. But I'm afraid that I've led us from our topic, so I'll be quiet."

At that point John Alex hoisted himself out of his chair and announced, "I've gut ta go out back an' have a word er two with Churchill, anabody else comin'?"

No one else wanted to join in on the conversation. Ann looked mystified.

Brother Thomas stroked his beard and said, "Frugal, help me here. Keystone species are those that play a unique role in ecosystem structure and process. Correct?"

Frugal nodded.

"So if these species are removed from the ecosystem the community would be different. Correct?

Frugal nodded again.

"Well, he mentioned moose and deer. How do they affect the ecosystem?"

Frugal smiled. "Let's say we have a forested area containing balsam fir, spruce, trembling aspen, birch, and moose. The moose prefer eating the hardwoods, but will eat balsam fir if nothing else is available. They seldom, if ever, eat spruce. By feeding on the nutrient-rich hardwood foliage they speed up the succession from hardwoods to softwood. In the long term, the acidity of the softwood foliage slows soil nutrient cycling as sites become more acidic. This in turn, changes soils from being bacteria dominated to fungal dominated, and so it goes. The concept of keystones is nebulous to say the least. Interrelationships are so complex that many species and mutualisms * can qualify as being a keystone. However, the rule that I go by is that any species or mutualism whose function isn't backed up by others is a good candidate for being considered as a keystone."

Jean suddenly announced that she was going in to Ming's to get a couple of pizzas and a box of beer. She was quickly joined by Doris and Ann. John Alex also thought that he should go along too as he could certainly stand a doughnut..er three, and since he felt a slight scratch in his throat, he'd better pick up a pint of black rum to fend off possible pneumonia and probable death.

"What kin I do ta enhance wildlife Frugal?"

"Well Roddie, I guess it depends what wildlife you want to enhance. But first, what do you mean by the word 'wildlife'?"

"Yiss, yiss, yer gettin' jist like yon one over there." He pointed at me. "Startin' jist after the Earth cooled! Wildlife iss rabbits an deer an' moose. Da ya thinks I'm stupid? I'm wearin' underwear thet's older then you."

"Yep," said John Alex as he went out the door. "Roddie wass around 'fore Noah put out ta sea, eh?"

After Frugal stopped laughing he explained to Roddie that wildlife really includes fish, amphibians, reptiles, mammals, and birds.

"Oh," said Roddie. "Yiss, yiss, I wass goin' ta mention them but ya interrupted me. So how kin I enhance 'em?"

"Well, there are lots of things you can do. Tell you what, Monday I'll get you a good publication on improving wildlife habitat. You read it and, if you like, I'll take a walk over your woodlot with you next Saturday.

"Yiss, yiss, sounds good ta me. We'll take the young fella here with us an' he can blather on 'bout silviculture an' at least he'll know thet when he's with us he won't git lost and wander 'round all day."

"Can I come too?" asked Stanley. "I'd like to look around that old foundation with my metal detector."

"Yiss, yiss, I s'pose."

Later when Jean, Doris, Ann, and John Alex returned, John Alex said, "Boys! The fog's ass thick ass mashed potatoes over in the village. Hed ta shake the Captain's hand a couple of times ta keep up me courage, eh?. Anaone want a swig?"

Everyone declined except Fred. "Ahh, yes, yes, I'll have a little dram John Alex." And with that he upped the pint and killed Captain Morgan.

"Ahh, yes, yes, rather pleasing to the palate. Many thanks my friend. By the way, there's a new pint in my raincoat inner pocket. It's now yours."

"Well," said John Alex. "Fer a man who reads picture books, yer alright, eh?"

We had our pizza, played a few games of 45's, and decided to call our verbal festival a day.

As we were saying our goodbyes, Ann said, "I've enjoyed myself. Thank you all. And Brother Thomas, you appreciate quotes, so here's one for you that I'm including in my book. It's from Chief Seattle in his 1855 address to President Franklin Pierce.

Human kind has not woven the web of life,
We are but the thread of it.
Whatever we do to the Earth, we do our selves.
All things are bound together, all things connect.
Whatever befalls the Earth befalls also the children of the Earth.

Brother Thomas smiled. "Bless you Ann. Here's an affirming little haiku from the 13th century by Ch shû that you can ponder and take home with you."

The moon is in the water;
Broken and broken again,
Still it is there.

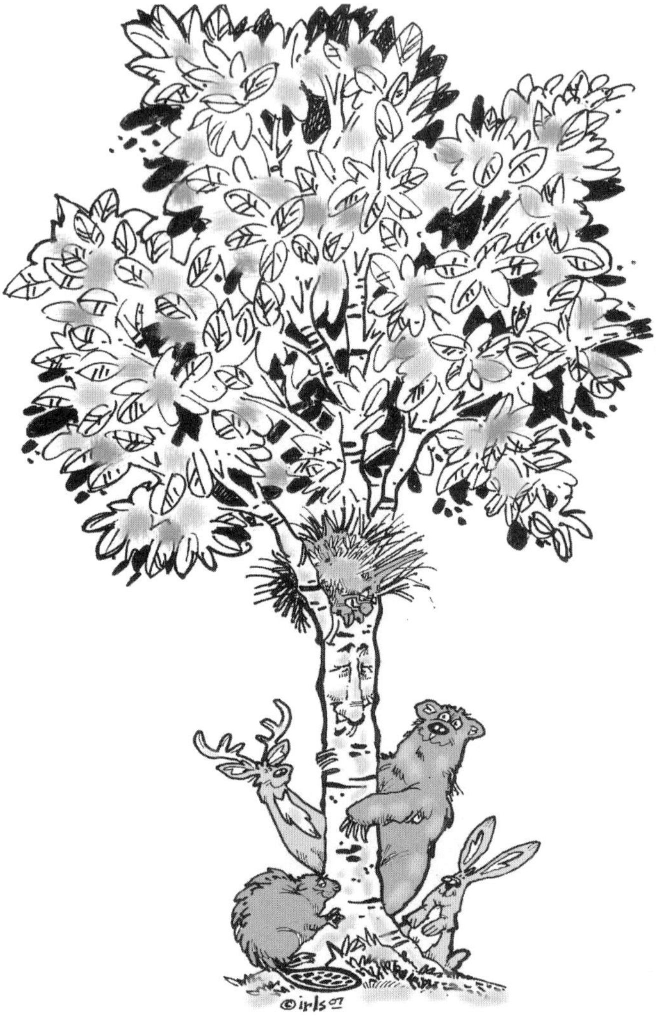

THE WATER, WILDLIFE, AND WOOD WALKABOUT

> *Here is the means to end the great extinction spasm. The next century will, I believe, be the era of restoration ecology.*
> - E.O. Wilson, 1992

Frugal picked me up at about 6:30 on Saturday morning. The day was cloudy and windy. All the better to keep the mosquitoes at bay.

Frugal and I are both interested in forest restoration, and on our drive over to get Roddie we talked about it.

"You know," said Frugal, "so far, ecosystems have an incredible resilience and have been able to recuperate from human exploitation. But every system has its limitations, and I think it's high time that we humans get over our feigned ignorance of environmental problems and wise up."

"Pretty strong statement for early in the morning my son," I replied. "But let me play the devil's advocate. The word restoration suggests that the destruction of habitats can be fixed. With this thinking, I'll not worry about habitat destruction in one area because I'll simply point out that degradation or destruction is being fixed in another area. This implies there's a 'balance' to overall loss."

"Yea," he replied. "Perhaps similar to the idea of carbon credits? However, restoration isn't mitigation. By restoration we're attempting to increase viable habitat by helping natural processes so they again become completely self-perpetuating."

"Something like boosting a dead battery so the vehicle can start and continue to operate?" I asked.

"Yes, I guess you could put it that way. And to my way of thinking, not only must degraded habitat be restored, we also have to include the conservation of existing viable habitat *before* we degrade it."

I glanced over at Frugal. "Think all this is possible on a spaceship that's currently occupied by a greedy crew of consumers that chooses to ignore the fact that they're actually sabotaging the craft itself?"

"For the sake of my boys, and perhaps someday my grandchildren, I really hope so. You're getting cynical."

"Nope, just discouraged and frustrated," I replied.

Roddie was standing looking at his garden when I turned into his driveway.

"Uncommonly fine large day, what?" He cried.

Frugal scowled at him. "It's cloudy and windy."

"So, what's yer point anaway? Yer up an' about ain't ya? Even if ya do gut a face longer then a wet week."

"Good point," I replied. "Let's head for the woods."

As we drove over to the Foxbrook Road woodlot Frugal cheered up and asked Roddie if he had read the wildlife material he had given him.

"Yiss, yiss," Roddie replied. "Good readin'. I gut a few ideas from yer stuff. Thanks. I'd like ta see more partridge, er ass ya calls 'em, ruffled grouse, some ducks, an' some fish in the pond. An' I'm goin' ta grow Shiitake mushrooms too."

"Good," Frugal replied. "But it's not ruffled, it's *ruffed* grouse."

"Jist testin' ya," said Roddie as he lit his pipe and filled the cab with acrid blue smoke.

Frugal coughed. Roddie broke wind. I put down the window. The universe was unfolding as it should as we drove up FoxbrookR-road.

Stanley's Volvo was parked in the gravel pit. He was nowhere to be seen. I had given him directions on how to find the old cellar excavation and assumed that we would find him there.

"Where do you want to start Roddie?" I asked.

"At the beginnin', when the Earth cooled. Where else does ya always start, ya gommice."

"Let's visit leech's pond first, then the stands you have on these photos," Frugal suggested as he nodded to me. "We can see what's there, talk about it and take some field notes for Roddie's management plan."

"An' jist when did anaone give ya the power ta name me pond? I already gut a name fer it. Kin ya guesses what it iss?"

"Skivvies pond? Perilous pool?" I guessed.

Frugal joined in. "Loch Ness? Clod-hopper pond?"

"Nope, yer all wrong. I named the pond 'Roddie's Pond'. Gut a nice ring ta it, don't ya thinks?"

"Yep," replied Frugal. "Original too."

Roddie nodded. 'Ya, I'm an original kind a guy. The wife calls me a snag. I thinks it means a sensitive new age guy. That er a dead standin' tree."

The pond's water was rippled by the wind. Swallows swooped over its surface. "How deep is your pond Roddie?" asked Frugal.

"Don't know an' I ain't goin' ta wade in an' see. Why do ya ask?"

"You said you wanted to stock it with fish. I like to see a stocked pond at least 8 feet (2.4 m) deep so it doesn't freeze to the bottom in the winter.

"Your pond is fed by the brook and by the spring up in the hardwood clearcut. That's good because these waters transport nutrients and insects into the pond and also oxygenate your pond's water."

"Yes, and Roddie," I said, "you'll have to do something about that so-called road that Cut-an' Run dozed. Every time it rains or some dimwit on an ATV or 4x4 uses it, a surge of silt flows into the brook. This silt is clogging the brook's gravel bottom that fish use for spawning."

"Silt also smothers fish eggs," Frugal added. "But back to the pond. If you're going to stock it there are some things to consider such as what species of fish you'll use. Will you net the fish to harvest them, or will you operate a U-Fish?

"And then there's the day-to-day operation. You'll need to haul feed in to the pond so you'll have to fix up that trail. You'll also need a shed to store your fish food, nets, and other things. Plus a

small dock would be nice. You could feed the fish from there.
Frugal stopped and frowned. "Then there's protection."

"What doess ya mean?" asked Roddie.

"There's a growing local osprey population and they'll quickly discover your fish, so you'll have to have some way to protect the fish from them. We'll add some suggestions and recommendations to your management plan."

Frugal looked around the pond. "I like to see hardwoods surrounding a pond like this for a number of reasons. They provide a windbreak for insects hovering over the water. Your fish will appreciate this as they feed on them. The leaf fall and twigs off trees also add nutrients to your pond. But, some hardwoods are better than others because some have a higher nutrient value. Aspen, maple, birch are good. Beech and oak aren't as good because their leaves are slow to decompose, and the oak leaves are also acidic. However, I do like to see willows and alders as they add bank stability.

"Perhaps we should develop some kind of a hardwood tree-species matrix for your management plan that indicates their watercourse, wildlife and economic value."

I pictured it in my mind. It could look like this.

Excellent – E Good - G Fair – F Not Applicable NA	Red oak	Yellow birch	Sugar maple	White ash	Beech	White birch	Red maple	Aspen	Pin cherry	Grey birch
Economic value	E	E	E	E	G	E/G	G	F	NA	NA
Watercourse Value	F	E	E	G	F	E	E	E	F	E
Songbirds	E	F	G	F	E	F	G	E	G	G
Upland game birds	E	G	F	F	F	G	F	E	F	F

| Fur and game animals | E | G | E | F | E | G | E | E | F | F |

My musing was cut short by what sounded like some ATV's off in the distance. Frugal scowled and turned to Roddie.

"We talked about protection from osprey predation, but don't forget protection from those suffering from a distinct discoloration of the neck region usually combined with a sign pinned to their forehead proclaiming *space for rent*."

"Huh? Oh, I gits it. Ya means red necks. The band a merry morons thet goess muddin', an' litterin', an' drinkin', an' smashin', an' stealin', and who thinks thet most a the words on their tattoos are spelt right. By the way, I caught Johnny Cut an' Run unloadin' an excavator in me gravel pit lass Sunday afternoon. Said he jist needed a few loads a pit-run gravel. Said he didn't see any harm in thet. Tole him ta git 'fore I sics the Mounties after 'im. Uncultivated, er what!"

"You should probably install a gate on the entrance to your pit. At least it'll keep the honest people out," said Frugal.

"What about the brook that flows into the pond?" I asked. "What should we do about that Frugal?"

"Wait a minute. Jist fer the record I named the brook 'Foxbrook'. Thought thet ya should know fer yer management plan."

"Foxbrook Road was named after Foxbrook River which is about two miles from here," I said.

"Yiss, yiss," he replied. "I knows thet, but there happened ta be two foxes an' two brooks in the area ya gommice. 'Pears ta me thet yer mind must be run by ropes an' pulleys an' ratchets. Not operatin' like a well-oiled abacus like me own, what?"

"Clever," nodded Frugal. "Yep, the evidence is overwhelming Roddie. You're beyond understanding."

"Could we please get back to talking about this brook?" I asked.

"Yes," said Frugal. "I'd like to take a walk from where the brook enters Roddie's pond back to it's source northwest of this woodlot. Ya don't happen to know who owns that property do you?"

"Northport Lumber," I replied. "They own a block of about 2,400 acres."

"Ok, why don't you and Roddie go and take a look at his silvicultural options; I'll walk the stream, see what condition it's in, then meet you back at the truck; say in a couple or three hours?"

"Yiss, yiss," piped up Roddie. "Ya go sloggin' up along the brook. Me an' him'll go cavortin' through Cut An' Run's slash."

And with that, Frugal left us, heading over towards the pond. I reached back and took out the aerial photos of Roddie's woodlot from the pocket in the back of my vest. Showing it to Roddie, I suggested that we visit stands ④: the 20-acre softwood clearcut; ⑤: the 30-acre hardwood clearcut; stand ⑥: the 15-acre mixedwood stand; ⑦: the 10-acre young softwood stand; and finally, stand ⑧: the 7-acre old burn. We could then return to the truck and meet up with Frugal and discuss some stream enhancement and wildlife options.

"Yiss, yiss, let's git on with it. Since the sun came out the black flies an' skiddas iss drainin' me dry. Give me some a yer fly dope 'fore I runs outta blood."

"What do you want to with this white spruce clearcut Roddie?"

"What kin I do?"

"One of two things. You can do nothing and let secondary succession revegetate the area. In that case you'll have grasses, herbaceous vegetation, raspberry, other shrubs, and shade intolerant hardwoods such as pin cherry, gray birch, aspen, and perhaps willow. You'll probably eventually get balsam fir, spruce, white pine, and red maple.

"The other option is to site prepare and plant seedlings. The slash will have to be moved around, perhaps by a skidder hauling anchors and chains. This will clear enough slash so you can actually plant the area.

"We're now getting into costs with site preparation, purchase of seedlings and planting them. Having invested this much money the planted seedlings must be protected from other vegetation competition until they're what we call free to grow. This usually requires at least one application of a herbicide.*"

"How many seedlin's do I needs ta buy?"

"Depends on how far apart that you plant them. If you plant 6' x 6' you're looking at, let's see, 43,560 divided by 36 equals 1,210, times 20 acres comes to 24,200 seedlings."

"What's the best thing fer me ta do?"

"Well," I replied, "That depends. From a long-term ecological sustainability point of view I believe that it's better to allow secondary succession to take its course. With the vegetation change from a softwood to herbaceous/hardwood growth there's a gradual cleansing of softwood soil pathogens*; an injection of 'compost' as the annual initial vegetation decomposes for a number of years; and a buffering of soil acidity. That's how Nature has been rebounding from disturbances for thousands of years."

"Minds me a crop rotation in farmin'. "

"That's right Roddie. However, from an economic view you would be losing thirty or so years when your ground could be growing a product such as pulpwood, studwood, or sawlogs.

"Having said all this, it comes down to what *you* want to do because it's your land; what you can afford to do, although you might qualify for government financial assistance; and, are you comfortable to follow up with any necessary treatments such as applying herbicides, insecticides, or manual weeding to protect the initial investment of preparing and planting the site."

"So what does ya suggest fer thiss stand?"

"If it was mine, I'd plant it. But I wouldn't establish a species-simple forest. I like to see more species diversity, so I'd plant a variety of tree species as long as those species were compatible to the site. And, not trying to confuse matters, I probably wouldn't plant much black spruce or jack pine."

"Why not?"

"Because of the uncertainty of climate change. If temperatures increase as they're expected to, black spruce, balsam fir, and jack pine will be stressed and won't do so well. Remember Roddie, what you plant next spring will probably be growing in a different climate by the time the trees are 80 to 100 years old. However, having said that, I'd still plant a variety of species other than those I just mentioned."

"I sees. Don't put all yer eggs inta one basket. Somethin' fer me ta think 'bout. Ok, let's get over ta the next stand an' git outta thiss friggin' slash."

As we entered the hardwood clearcut we could hear someone talking but couldn't see anyone. When we reached the old cellar the mystery was solved. There in the depression sat Stanley and John Alex. Beside them lay Stanley's metal detector.

John Alex noticed us first. He held up and waved a rust-encased object, then tossed it to Roddie.

"It's an old flint lock pistol, eh? Stanley's huntin' machine jist tole us where ta dig an' bingo! There is wass, eh? An' look at the collection we already gut. It's over there on thet rock in the corner, eh?"

Roddie and I went down into the old cellar hole and examined Stanley's find. There was the head of a large broad axe, about 10 rusted blacksmith-made square nails, and the badly rusted remains of a long knife.

Stanley stood up and smiled. He was about to say something when Roddie said, "Stanley, ya should otta wear a cap on account a because yer bald head iss shinin' like the bottom of a copper pot. Ain't healthy ta git cooked like thet. Ya should git yerself a railroad cap like meself."

Stanley frowned. "First, you're probably right about the sunburn, but it's a scientific fact that you can't grow both hair *and* brains. Second, I don't have wrinkles. You however, have so many that you can screw your cap on for windy weather."

The cords on Roddie's neck bulged out like chicken legs, but he said nothing. John Alex and I chuckled.

"What I was going to say before Roddie offered his profound observation and advice was that I've done some research on this old cellar. Turns out that this land was once occupied by a guy named William Nathaniel Leader, his wife Matilda, and six children. Records show that on June 30, 1743, the body of William was found. He had apparently shot himself. There was no further mention of his wife and family so I suspect that they probably moved away."

"Interestin', eh? Ta think thet we're holdin' somethin' in our hand thet wass here fer about three hundred years. An' a flint lock pistol at thet, eh?"

"Yiss, yiss, but we gut ta be goin'."

Roddie and I walked across the clearcut hardwood stand. Except for the smashed and downed small-diameter sugar maples it was easy walking.

"What does ya suggest thet I does here?"

"As I always say, you have at least two options. Do something, or do nothing. In this case you could plant softwood seedlings or do nothing. If you plant softwoods they'll certainly grow, but you'll have to herbicide the expected hardwood regrowth. Personally, I don't agree with clearcutting a shade-tolerant hardwood stand, but in your case you're faced with a 30-acre hardwood clearcut. If it were mine, I'd do nothing for three or four years. I'd wait to see how the stand regenerates itself. Depending on summer conditions, I expect some, or if we're really lucky, many of the hardwood seedlings to survive; and, although there are many large diameter stumps which won't provide many stump sprouts, there are quite a few smaller diameter sugar maple stumps that will. In time this coppice regrowth can be managed."

"So ya thinks thet I should wait an' see?"

"Yep, that's my opinion."

"Then let's hustle our buns on ta the next stand."

We hustled our buns.

Stand ⑤ was the 35-year old, 15-acre mixedwood stand consisting of balsam fir, red spruce, red maple, yellow birch and scattered aspen. I'd been thinking about this stand since I previously visited it. It appeared to be growing well and I didn't see the need for any immediate intervention. Perhaps in 15 or 20 years a species cut could be done to remove the balsam fir and aspen. However, I kept these thoughts to myself and asked Roddie what he thought he should do.

"Nothin'," he replied. "These trees are jist young adults an' I've gut other more important things ta do. I'd jist ass soon let 'em be happy an' grow fer now."

I couldn't have said it better. Sad, eh?

As we were walking over to stand ⑦, Roddie said, "I've gut a question fer ya. Yer always harpin' 'bout dead wood, so how much iss enough?"

"That's a difficult question to answer because it depends on the size and species of the downed logs. The larger logs naturally last longer, yet species makes a difference too. For example, aspen decomposes faster than cedar or tamarack. But researchers have come up with some idea of how much is enough. They tell us that about 20 – 30 cubic metres, or, put simply, about a truckload per hectare should be sufficient. However, when you look at a healthy old-growth forest you'll find as much as 30% dead wood in the overall woody biomass. For now, and for the sake of simplicity, I'll stick to the truckload per hectare because I can visualize that much downed wood over that much area. Is that clear Roddie?"

"Clear ass mud, but I guesses thet I understands."

Stand ⑦ was the dense young fir-spruce stand. I remembered that the stem count was about 12 000 stems per hectare and mentioned this to Roddie.

"I don't wants ta hear nothin' 'bout metric. Talk to me in the English of good ole King George the turd er go home."

"Perhaps you should pick a King George with another number, but anyhow, to convert

12 000 stems per hectare to stems per acre just divide by 2.471. I did it on a back page of my field book and told Roddie that it works out to be 4,856 stems per acre.

"So what doess ya suggest?"

"Again, what's done is up to you. If it were mine, I'd space the stand to encourage diameter growth on the uncut trees. I'd reduce the number of stems per acre from 4,800 to about 1,200. This would lessen the present competition for light, water, and nutrients and allow your chosen crop trees to get bigger. I'd also favour the red spruce over the balsam fir because the spruce is a longer-lived species. This would in effect raise the percentage of spruce in the post-spaced stand."

"What would ya do with all the trees ya cut?"

"Nothing. Just make sure they're down on the ground. There they'll gradually decompose and add to the stand's organic component."

"What 'bout the maple, birch an' pin cherries?"

"For diversity I'd want to keep about 15 to 30 percent of the stand in hardwoods. Your red maple clumps are coppice growth. I'd thin each clump down to two stems making sure that these stems are located low on the side of the original stump. I'd leave as much birch as possible keeping in mind that my softwood crop trees can't be too close to the birch because young birches tend to whip around in the wind. I'd also leave all the pin cherries. They provide food for birds, annual leaf litter, and are a short-lived species."

"Ok, let's beat our feet over ta the old burn an' see what's ta be done there. An' 'fore ya says it, I kin always do nothin'."

Roddie's plan for the woodlot included enhancing habitat for ruffed grouse. Frugal and I had discussed it and he had suggested that stand ⑧, the old burn with all the aspen, would be ideal for that purpose.

As we neared stand ⑧ I asked Roddie why he's interested in grouse and ducks. He stopped, lifted an eyebrow and said, "Cause I likes em ya gommice. An' quite callin' em ruffed grouse, they're partridge ya numb twit."

Well, I guess the why wasn't up for discussion. Just the how. I wondered what was apparently bothering Roddie but didn't dare ask. Perhaps I'd find out later.

"Ok Roddie, here's Frugal's recommendation for improving your *partridge* habitat. Aspen stands are their favorite habitat, especially in the spring when they eat the catkins on the male trees."

"Stop the bus! Yer tellin' me thet there are boy trees an' girl trees?"

"Yep, and it gets better than that Roddie. Common male and female trees, which by the way are called dioecious, that we have around here include trembling aspen, large-tooth aspen, balsam poplar, and ash. However, red maples have both male and female flowers that are often found on different branches.

"Our common softwoods, and hardwoods such as the birches, beech and red oak are called monoecious which means that both sexes are on the same tree. Usually the female sex parts are above the pollen-producing male sex parts to lessen the chance of self pollination.

"But then there are hermaphrodite trees such as pin cherry that bear perfect flowers that have both male and female reproductive parts in the same flower; or how about polygamous trees such as sugar maple that bear both perfect flowers and imperfect flowers that lack either the male or female reproductive parts."

"Yiss, yiss Nature's gut a lot a different ways ta hev sex. Prob'ly near ass many ass Jin Alek. Lass week he wass tellin' me thet he an' Martha joined the mile-high club, but I don't imagin' thet the broom closet above Ming's Ptomaine Palace counts fer much… Jest kiddin'. Poor ole Jin Alex ain't be doin' the testosterone two-step since Noah dropped anchor on top a thet mountain."

"Let's get back to aspen and partridges. You have 7 acres of the old burn on your property and Frugal suggests that you can manage this stand for ruffed grouse by gradually dividing it into three growth stages of about two and a quarter acres each. Your objective will be to develop a two and a quarter acre area aged 2 to 9 years to act as brood cover; another area aged 10 to 24 years old to be an overwintering and breeding place; and the last area being over 25 years old and to be used as nesting and feeding habitat. By that time they'll also probably nest over in the adjacent softwood stand that you spaced."

"Yiss, yiss, so how doess I do this?"

"The stand is now 10 years old, so after the leaves are off this fall you could begin to establish your next age class by clearcutting two and a quarter acres. Being cut in the autumn will ensure that there'll be an abundant number of aspen suckers next year.

This leaves you with an uncut area of about four and three quarters acres. In 15-years time you'll clearcut half this area. This means you'll have one area in the 25-year age class, one in the 15-year age class and the regenerating area that you cut that year."

"Yiss, yiss, I sees. How's 'bout puttin' a sketch of the stand in the management plan an' puttin' the year of each cut on it so's I kin follow it. Anathin' else?"

"Well, not really. The only other thing I can suggest is to paint a red band on some of the aspens in the area that's going to be your oldest aged habitat. Do this in the spring when the catkins are visible. You could then cut some trees competing with these male aspens to encourage their growth and fuller development."

"Ok let's head out an' see what Frugal iss up ta."

As we were walking out Roddie asked me what he could do to encourage more ducks, especially wood ducks and black ducks.

"I also asked Frugal that question Roddie. He said that your pond is certainly a good candidate for use by waterfowl for a number of reasons. First, it's large enough; second, the east side has that shallow area that's great for aquatic plants; and third, there's surrounding grass, shrub and young tree cover for ground-nesting ducks but you also want to encourage wood ducks and these are cavity-nesting birds. However, you don't have any large old hardwoods or softwoods surrounding your pond. Frugal suggested that you could build some nesting boxes for them."

"An' jist what doess I nail these boxes to?"

"This winter you could go out on the ice, chop some holes, pound in some poles and nail your boxes to these poles."

"Oy, yiss, yiss, I sees. I should a thunk a thet. Do ya suppose the leeches 'ill be a problem?"

I stared at Roddie.

"Jist foolin'. But changin' the subject, I hed a funny feelin' come over me when Jin Alek throwed me thet ole pistol. I jist knowed thet I wass holdin' the gun thet what's hiss name shot hisself with. Felt some queer. Still doess, so I'm goin' ta change the name a me pond from Roddie's Pond to Leader's Pond an' the brook from Foxbrook ta Matilda's Brook. Don't know where these settlers are buried, but at least this'll keep their mem'ry alive...ta me anaway."

As we emerged out into the gravel pit I could see Frugal sitting on the tailgate of my truck. His head was lowered and he was writing in his field book. He looked up and waved.

When we got to the truck Roddie had to immediately go into great detail about the finding of the pistol and the fact that he felt queer.

Frugal smirked. "Never thought of you as that Roddie."

Roddie stared at him with a blank expression. "Well I doess. Anaway, what did ya find?"

"I'll get back to the section of the brook that's on your woodlot in a minute. I followed the brook a long way over Northport Lumber's woodland. They've done a lot of harvesting in the area but have left a good riparian * or buffer strip * along both sides of the brook. They bridged the brook once with a nice bridge and appear to have done minimal disturbance."

"I'm not surprised, I said. "Northport Lumber is a well-run, environmentally-conscious company. But on the other end of the scale we have Johnny Cut An' Run. What damage did he do and how does Roddie fix it?"

"Johnny and his crew damaged your section of the brook in three ways. First, he cut right up to the edge of the waterway. By law he was supposed to leave a minimum of 50 feet of uncut woods. Second, his skidder drove across the brook in a number of places, and it sure looks like he skidded logs through the brook in two places because the banks are cut down badly. Just mud left. And third, he dozed his so-called road right next to the brook in some places. Naturally, any muddy water flows into the waterway. I was just sitting here writing notes for a ticket for Cut An' Run when you guys came. He'll be dealt with in court.

"Anyway, I followed the brook to its source, and you should see it! It's the biggest spring* I ever saw. Just boiling out of the ground like a 12-inch geyser. And as cold as ice! What a spring."

I nodded. "Aqua vitae...the water of life."

"'Fore youse guys gits too sentimental how's 'bout tellin' me what ta do with my bit a the brook."

Frugal was just going to talk about brook restoration when he was interrupted by a cry from the trail that led into the pond. We turned and saw John Alex actually *running* towards us.

"Stanley's hunting machine jist found a dead person. Takes two ta tangle, eh?"

"What!" exclaimed Roddie. "First ya better set an' git yer wind 'fore ya dies yerself and then ya kin tell us 'bout it. It prob'ly ain't goin' no where."

After John Alex regained his breath he told us that Stanley's metal detector had made a loud buzzing as he again swept it over the area where they had dug up the flint lock pistol. Digging deeper they uncovered a human skull. Next to it they found a rusted meat cleaver.

"An', holy jumpin," said John Alex, "there weren't anamore bones. Jist the skull, eh? An' it had a hole in it clear through the forehead part, eh?"

"Jeedee jumpin' Christopher," cried Roddie. "We gut ourselves an ole-time murder. Let's go an' hev a look."

As Frugal, Roddie, and John Alex rushed across the pit to the trail I radioed the office and asked the secretary to call the RCMP and ask them to meet me at the gravel pit on Foxbrook Road. Not wanting to say what we found over the air, I told her there has been an accident that they should check out.

"Was anyone hurt?" Do you need an ambulance?"

"Ah...no. Just the cops...over and out."

Corporal Sullivan arrived in about 10 minutes. I like Tom and he's respected in Big Spoon Cove and surrounding area because he has common sense. If he thinks that the situation warrants it, he'll go by the spirit of the law rather than the letter of the law. Not like some of the other younger members who try to build up their reputations by the number of charges and convictions they accumulate. He stepped out of the cruiser and came over to where I was sitting on my truck's tailgate and asked what was the problem.

"Nothing too serious," I replied. "Just an old human skeleton... or at least part of one."

As he and I made our way up to the old cellar site I filled Tom in on what had happened. When we reached the depression Stanley, John Alex and Roddie were sitting on the bank deep in discussion about what they had found. The skull lay in top of a pile of dirt that had been excavated from the hole.

Tom thanked Stanley and John Alex for bringing this to his attention and then told them to leave the cellar. He said that even though it was hundreds of years old it was still a crime scene and he would call in a forensic anthropologist to see if it could be determined what had happened.

"Go back about your business and say nothing to anyone. We don't want the whole village in here nosing around to see what's going on. And Stanley, you can gather up the old rusty nails. I'll keep all the other stuff you found in case it's needed in our investigation."

With that, we five headed back out to the pit. Stanley and John Alex left for home and Frugal, Roddie and I looked at each other.

"Yiss, yiss, where wass we anaway?"

"Frugal was going to give you some tips on how to restore your part of the brook."

"Yiss, yiss but keep it simple taday. Ya kin go inta more detail when ya writes me plan. Thiss murder gut me beat ta a snot. If'n me arse wass draggin' any lower, I'd hev ta tuck it inta the cuff a me overalls. Thet er duct tape it ta me left leg."

Frugal laughed. He must have had a mental image of Roddie, who was at thin as a communion wafer, with his non-existent butt firmly attached to his skinny left leg with grey duct tape. A sobering sight indeed.

"Apart from the damage that Cut An' Run caused, this brook is in pristine condition. Although Northport Lumber has done extensive harvesting on their land, they've taken proper stream protection measures, so the brook wasn't affected.

"I had mentioned three types of damage that occurred. First, there was cutting done up to the edge of the brook. Where hardwoods were cut there are already stump sprouts about a foot tall. In time these'll grow and provide shade for the brook. But in areas where softwood has been growing and were cut, you should plant some seedlings such as maple, ash, white pine or willow. Probably the easiest to plant in moist areas is willow because you can simply take cuttings from branches and stick them vertically along the banks of the brook. They'll root and grow quickly, thus not only providing shade and leaf fall, but they'll also help stabilize the bank from erosion.

"The second problem is the skidding or forwarding of wood through the brook. Significant damage was done to the banks and they're now eroding into the watercourse. There are two things you can do. First you'll have to armour and protect the banks with either rock, or logs and rock. If rocks are used they should be large enough to resist the force of spring floods. You want them to stay in place and not go tumbling down the brook. If you choose to use logs and rock, the logs should also be large and sturdy enough. They can be pinned in place with rebar. After that, large rock should be placed at the bottom, behind, and above these logs. The muddy areas above the high water mark should be covered no later than mid-summer with late-cut hay to both protect the area from rain and provide a seed source for grasses and wildflowers.

"The third problem is that damn so-called road. Where it's adjacent to the brook you'll have to get something growing on it. If you plant tree seedlings on it they'll probably frost heave in the spring. Because of this I suggest that for now you cover these areas with seed hay. When a sod cover is established you could probably plant some large tree seedlings.

"Apart from that, the only thing you should be aware of is the importance of large woody material that's in the brook. Leave it. It provides shelter and protection for fish and helps to create pools because water flowing over the log scours a pool on the downstream side.

"We could get into other remedial measures such as digger logs, cover logs, and in-stream deflectors, but these aren't needed in your case."

"Yiss, yiss, sounds like somethin' me an' the current first wife an' former sweetheart kin do. Let's go home."

On our way home Roddie, puffing with great vigor on that blasted pipe asked Frugal if fish could smell and hear.

"Trout have a well-developed sense of smell Roddie and as for hearing they don't have any ears."

"Humph...guesses they couldn't wear glasses then."

"I said they didn't have any ears but they can still detect sound because they have an inner ear that perceives vibrations, and also, low frequency sounds are detected by their lateral line."

"Lateral line, iss thet somethin' like a plimsoll line *?"

"Yeah, I guess so Roddie. There are a line of special scales that have small holes located along the body of the fish. They're connected to nerve endings that can detect sound, change in pressure, and also movement."

"I sees."

As we pulled into Roddie's driveway he said, "I wants ta thank youse guys fer all thet ya done fer me. Ya both gut yer work cut out fer ya if ya expects ta change a society a consumers inta a society a conservers. But I guesses thet somebody gut ta try...good luck fer the sake a Nature an' mankind. Didn't think thet I could philosophize too did ya, ya gommices. Be brave but carry a big stick."

And with that blessing Roddie got out of the truck.

"Amen," said Frugal.

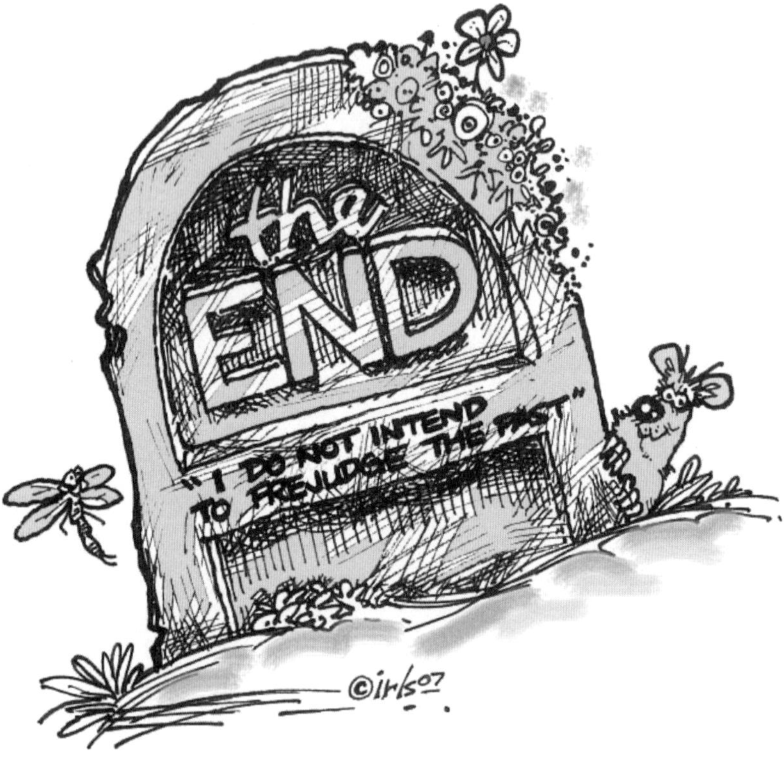
the END
"I DO NOT INTEND TO PREJUDGE THE PAST"

EPILOGUE

Word got out that bones had been found on Roddie's new woodlot. The RCMP engaged Dr. Anna Kelsey, a forensic anthropologist to investigate and report on the findings. The entire bottom of the depression was dug up and what was found was sad indeed. They found a skeletal remains without a head, and the remains of six children ranging in age from a year to eight years old. The children's skulls showed that they had died violently. They were viciously bludgeoned to death.

The skeleton without a head was examined in the lab and by measurement it was determined that it was female, aged about 37 years. They had discovered Matilda and children.

Roddie requested that the bones that had been removed for identification be reburied in the depression. A committal service was held that was attended by many from Big Spoon Cove and surrounding area as the bones were re-laid to rest.

The following spring, and at his own expense, Roddie had a large granite boulder hauled to the site. To it he attached a plaque which told the sad story. Across the bottom of the plaque was a quote by William Whitelaw that read, "I do not intend to prejudge the past." Probably good advice.

P.S...Roddie received his written plan for the restoration of Roddie's New Woodlot.

APPENDIX A
IDENTIFICATION
OF SITE FACTORS

Source: Forestry Field Handbook: Province of Nova Scotia, Department of Natural Resources, 1993.
Reprinted with permission.

APPENDIX A   IDENTIFICATION OF SITE FACTORS

Drainage →

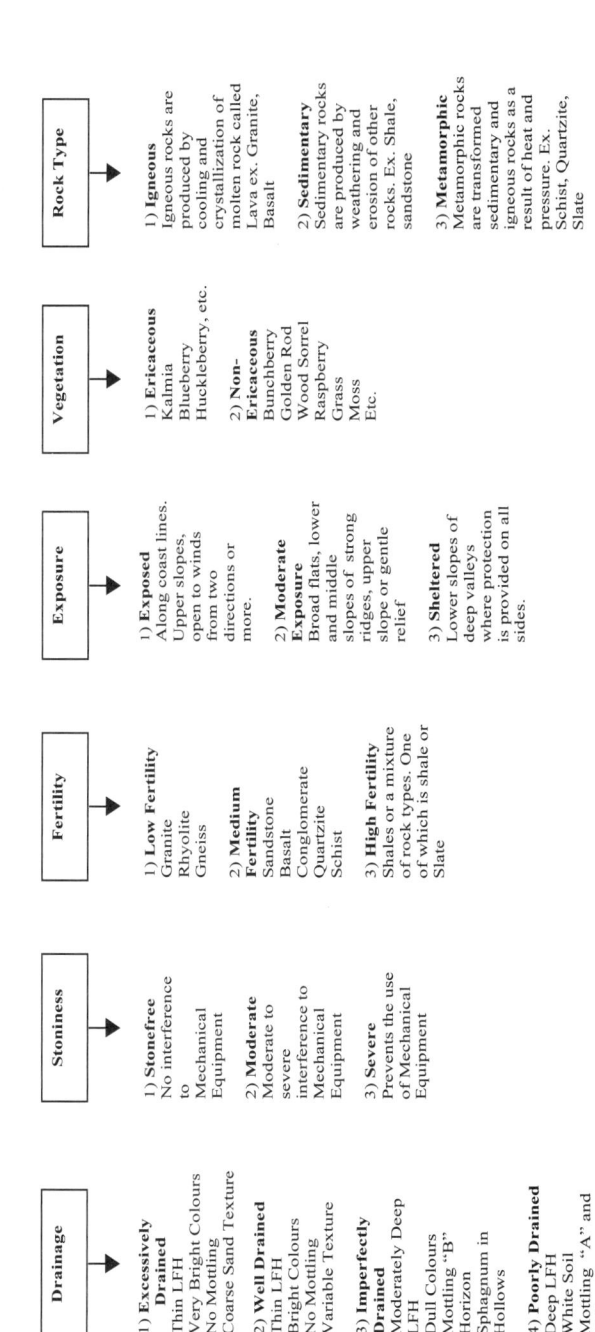

1) **Excessively Drained**
Thin LFH
Very Bright Colours
No Mottling
Coarse Sand Texture

2) **Well Drained**
Thin LFH
Bright Colours
No Mottling
Variable Texture

3) **Imperfectly Drained**
Moderately Deep LFH
Dull Colours
Mottling "B" Horizon
Sphagnum in Hollows

4) **Poorly Drained**
Deep LFH
White Soil
Mottling "A" and "B"
Sphagnum Common

Stoniness →

1) **Stonefree**
No interference to Mechanical Equipment

2) **Moderate**
Moderate to severe interference to Mechanical Equipment

3) **Severe**
Prevents the use of Mechanical Equipment

Fertility →

1) **Low Fertility**
Granite
Rhyolite
Gneiss

2) **Medium Fertility**
Sandstone
Basalt
Conglomerate
Quartzite
Schist

3) **High Fertility**
Shales or a mixture of rock types. One of which is shale or Slate

Exposure →

1) **Exposed**
Along coast lines. Upper slopes, open to winds from two directions or more.

2) **Moderate Exposure**
Broad flats, lower and middle slopes of strong ridges, upper slope or gentle relief

3) **Sheltered**
Lower slopes of deep valleys where protection is provided on all sides.

Vegetation →

1) **Ericaceous**
Kalmia
Blueberry
Huckleberry, etc.

2) **Non-Ericaceous**
Bunchberry
Golden Rod
Wood Sorrel
Raspberry
Grass
Moss
Etc.

Rock Type →

1) **Igneous**
Igneous rocks are produced by cooling and crystallization of molten rock called Lava ex. Granite, Basalt

2) **Sedimentary**
Sedimentary rocks are produced by weathering and erosion of other rocks. Ex. Shale, sandstone

3) **Metamorphic**
Metamorphic rocks are transformed sedimentary and igneous rocks as a result of heat and pressure. Ex. Schist, Quartzite, Slate

APPENDIX B
SOIL TEXTURE ASSESSMENT GUIDE

SOIL TEXTURE ASSESSMENT TESTS

Moist Cast Test: Compress some moist soil by clenching it in your hand; if the soil holds together (i.e., forms a cast), then test the strength of the cast by tossing it from hand to hand. The more durable it is, the more clay is present.

Ribbon Test: Moist soil is rolled into cigarette shape and then squeezed out between the thumb and forefinger to form the longest and thinnest ribbon possible.

FEEL TEST:

Graininess Test: Soil is rubbed between thumb and fingers to assess the % sand. Sand feels grainy.

Stickiness Test: Soil is wetted and compressed between the thumb and forefinger. Degree of stickiness is determined by noting how strongly it adheres to the thumb and forefinger upon release of pressure and how much it stretches.

Shine Test: A small amount of moderately dry soil is rolled into a ball and rubbed once or twice against a hard, smooth object such as a knife blade or thumbnail. A shine on the ball indicates clay in the soil.

Modified from the Canada Soil Information system (CanSIS) 1982.
Source: Forestry Field Handbook: Province of Nova Scotia, Department of Natural Resources, 1993.

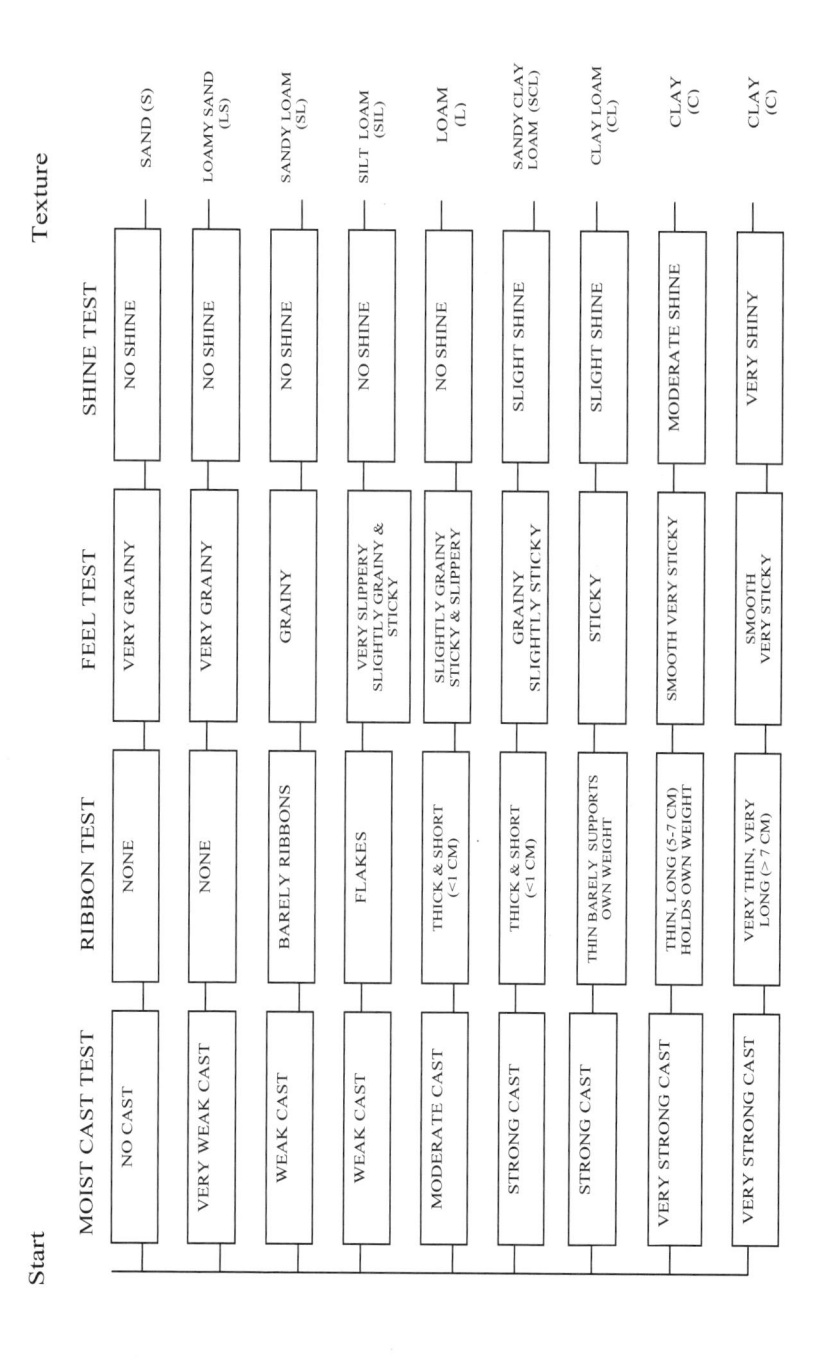

APPENDIX B SOIL TEXTURE ASSESSMENT GUIDE

Start → MOIST CAST TEST → RIBBON TEST → FEEL TEST → SHINE TEST → Texture

MOIST CAST TEST	RIBBON TEST	FEEL TEST	SHINE TEST	Texture
NO CAST	—	VERY GRAINY	NO SHINE	SAND (S)
VERY WEAK CAST	NONE	VERY GRAINY	NO SHINE	LOAMY SAND (LS)
WEAK CAST	BARELY RIBBONS	GRAINY	NO SHINE	SANDY LOAM (SL)
WEAK CAST	FLAKES	VERY SLIPPERY SLIGHTLY GRAINY & STICKY	NO SHINE	SILT LOAM (SIL)
MODERATE CAST	THICK & SHORT (<1 CM)	SLIGHTLY GRAINY STICKY & SLIPPERY	NO SHINE	LOAM (L)
STRONG CAST	THICK & SHORT (<1 CM)	GRAINY SLIGHTLY STICKY	SLIGHT SHINE	SANDY CLAY LOAM (SCL)
STRONG CAST	THIN BARELY SUPPORTS OWN WEIGHT	STICKY	SLIGHT SHINE	CLAY LOAM (CL)
VERY STRONG CAST	THIN, LONG (5–7 CM) HOLDS OWN WEIGHT	SMOOTH VERY STICKY	MODERATE SHINE	CLAY (C)
VERY STRONG CAST	VERY THIN, VERY LONG (>7 CM)	SMOOTH VERY STICKY	VERY SHINY	CLAY (C)

APPENDIX C
SPECIES/SITE SELECTION PLANTING KEY

Source: Forestry Field Handbook: Province of Nova Scotia, Department of Natural Resources, 1993

Reprinted with permisson.

APPENDIX C SPECIES/SITE SELECTION PLANTING KEY

Planting Season

- **Spring**: Delay planting Larches until after last frost
- **Fall**: rS not recommended after 1 August

Porcupine Hazard

- **Moderate – High**: WS or BS only
- **Low - Nil**

Hylobius Hazard

- **Moderate - High**: Swd – Mwd cut → Age of Cutover
  - 1 to 2 Years: Planting not recommended
  - 3 Years +
- **Low - Nil**: Hwd Cut

Eco Climate

- **Exposed**: RS is not recommended
- **Coastal**: RP is not recommended
- **Other**
- **Frost Pocket**: NS* is not recommended

*Delay planting of other species until after last frost

Region

- **C.B.H. ****: RS, WP, RP, JP, EL not recommended
- **All Other**

** Unique eco-climate only special provenances of WS, BS recommended

Vegetation Competition

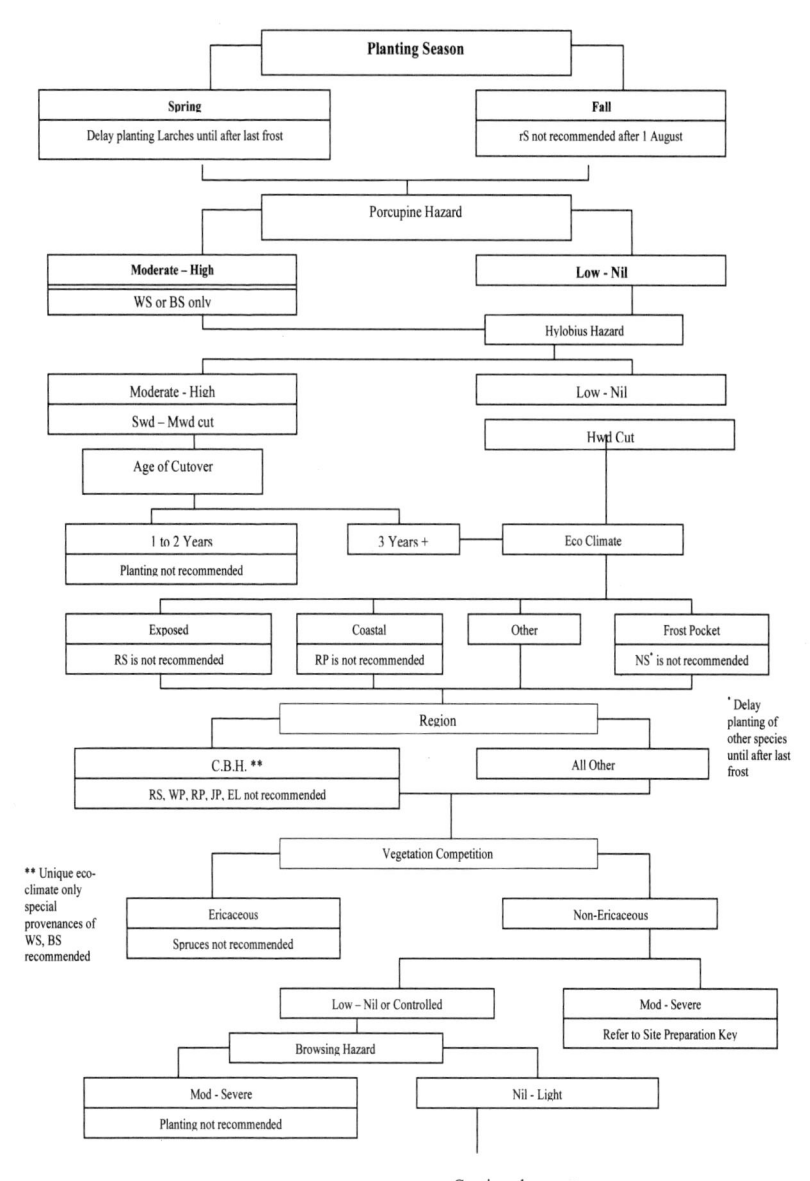

- **Ericaceous**: Spruces not recommended
- **Non-Ericaceous**

Browsing Hazard

- **Low – Nil or Controlled**
  - **Mod - Severe**: Planting not recommended
  - **Nil - Light**
- **Mod - Severe**: Refer to Site Preparation Key

Continued on next page

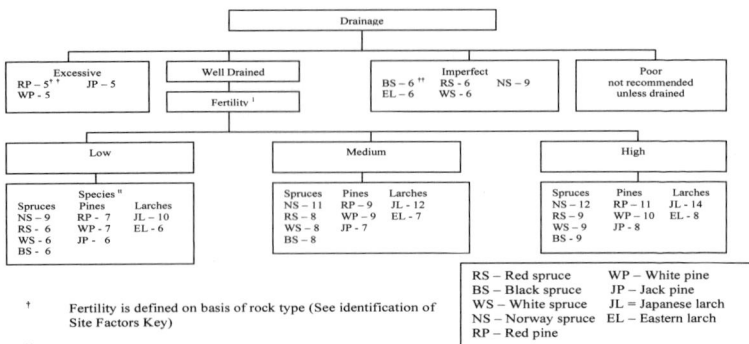

```
                              ┌─────────────────────┐
                              │      Drainage       │
                              └─────────────────────┘
         Excessive              Well Drained            Imperfect              Poor
    RP – 5††   JP – 5                              BS – 6 ††  RS - 6  NS – 9   not recommended
    WP - 5                         Fertility¹      EL – 6     WS - 6           unless drained
```

	Low			Medium			High	
	Species ⁿ		Spruces	Pines	Larches	Spruces	Pines	Larches
Spruces	Pines	Larches	NS – 11	RP – 9	JL - 12	NS – 12	RP – 11	JL - 14
NS – 9	RP - 7	JL – 10	RS – 8	WP – 9	EL - 7	RS – 9	WP – 10	EL - 8
RS - 6	WP - 7	EL - 6	WS – 8	JP - 7		WS – 9	JP - 8	
WS - 6	JP - 6		BS – 8			BS - 9		
BS - 6								

RS – Red spruce   WP – White pine
BS – Black spruce   JP – Jack pine
WS – White spruce   JL = Japanese larch
NS – Norway spruce   EL – Eastern larch
RP – Red pine

†   Fertility is defined on basis of rock type (See identification of Site Factors Key)

††   The expected gross merchantable mean annual increment (m^3 ha^{-1} yr^{-1}) is indicted for each species. For plantations established on sites with severe root competition (ericaceous vegetation or grass), expected productivity will be 1 to 3 m^3 ha^{-1} yr^{-1} less.

Note: Ericaceous sites revert to non-ericaceous with adequate site preparation.

APPENDIX D
DESIRABLE STOCKING AFTER THINNING

Desired DBH at Harvest	Number of Trees Per Acre		
	Softwood	Mixedwood	Hardwood
6"	1137	853	569
7"	857	643	429
8"	671	503	336
9"	541	405	270
10"	446	334	223
11"	374	281	187
12"	319	239	159
13"	275	207	138
14"	240	180	120
15"	212	159	106
16"	188	141	94
17"	168	126	84
18"	152	114	76
19"	137	103	69
20"	125	94	62

Source: Government of Canada/Province of Nova Scotia. *The Trees Around Us*. Printed in Canada, 1980

GLOSSARY

The limits of my language mean the limits of my world.
    - Ludwig Wittgenstein

Abiotic: Pertaining to the nonliving parts of an **ecosystem** such as soil particles, bedrock, air, water

Age:

Breast height age: The number of annual rings between the pith and bark. These are counted at breast height (4.5 ft. or 1.37 m) from the ground.

Stump age: The number of annual rings between the pith and bark counted across the top of a stump.

Harvest age: The number of years from establishment to economic maturity.

Longevity: The total age from establishment to the natural death of a tree.

Age class: A distinct aggregation of trees originating from a disturbance, or a grouping of trees i.e., 10-year age class, as used in management.

Age since release (also called **effective age**: The years since a tree was released from suppression.

Advance regeneration: Seedlings or saplings that develop or are present in the understory.

Adventitious: A part that develops outside the usual order of time, position or tissue.

Aspect: A position facing a particular direction i.e., a southerly aspect faces south.

Azimuth: The angle of a point measured clockwise from north.

Biological Diversity: The variety and abundance of life forms, processes, functions, and structures of plants, animals, and other living organisms,, including the relative complexity of species, communities, gene pools, and ecosystems at spatial scales that range from local through regional to global.

Biotic: Pertaining to living organisms and their ecological and physiological relations.

Bole: The main stem of a tree.

Bore a tree: Aging a tree by using an increment borer. This is an auger-like instrument with a hollow bit and extractor and used to extract thin cylinders of wood so that annual growth rings of the tree can be counted.

Browse: 1. Any woody vegetation consumed, or fit for consumption, by livestock or wild animals, mainly ungulates.
2. To forage or graze on the buds, stems, and leaves of woody growth.

Buffer: A vegetation strip or management zone of varying size, shape, and character maintained along a stream, lake, road, recreation site, or different vegetative zone to mitigate the impacts of actions on adjacent lands.

Carnivore: An organism that consumes animals or parts of animals.

Clone: Offspring genetically identical to its parent.

Community: An assemblage of plants and animals living together and occupying a given area.

Coppice: The production of new stems from a stump or roots.

GLOSSARY

Crown The part of a tree or woody plant bearing live branches and foliage.
Den: A wild animal's home.
Diameter: The diameter of the stem of a tree. This is usually measured at breast height (4.5 ft. or 1.37 m from the ground).
Distribution: How trees are situated on a unit area. Usually described as sparse, scattered, uniform, or dense.
Dormancy: A condition in the life of a seed when growth and development are temporarily suspended.
Dot grid: A transparent sheet of film with systematically arranged dots, each dot representing a number of area units (acres, hectares).
Downed woody material (DWM): Any piece(s) of dead woody material on the ground in forests or in streams.
Drainage: The soil characteristics that affect natural drainage. Soils are generally classified as excessively drained, well drained, imperfectly drained, or poorly drained.
Duff: The duff is made up of three layers. Also known as the LF & H. The duff consists of the surface layer or **litter** which contains leaves, needles, twigs, stems, bark, fruits and dead organisms. Beneath the litter layer is the **fermentation** layer where needles, leaves, twigs, etc., are in the process of decomposition. The lowest layer in the duff is the **humus** layer. This is the organic layer left after total decomposition. The humus is Nature's compost.
Ecosystem: A spatially explicit, relatively homogeneous unit of the earth that includes all interacting organisms and components of the **abiotic** environment within its boundaries.
Elements: Nitrogen, calcium, potassium, phosphorus, magne-

sium, sulphur, boron, chlorine, manganese, iron, copper, zinc, molyboenum, nickel and vandium.

Ericaceous vegetation: Species belonging to the Heath family. Includes bog rosemary, bearberry, leatherleaf, trailing arbutus, creeping snowberry, wintergreen, bog laurel, Labrador tea, cranberry, blueberry.

Even-aged stand: A stand of trees composed of a single age class in which the range of tree ages is usually ± 20 percent of rotation.

Exposure: The degree of being protected or unprotected from high winds.

Fauna The animal species present in a particular geographical region.

Flora The plant species in a given area.

Fungivore: An organism that eats fungi.

Germinant: A seed in the process of **germination**.

Germination: The development of a seedling from a seed.

Habitat; The place, natural or otherwise (including climate, food, cover, and water) where an animal, plant or population naturally or normally lives and develops.

Hardwood stand:Contains 0 – 25% softwood.

Herbaceous vegetation: ,A class of vegetation dominated by non-woody plants such as grasses, ferns and forbs (any broad-leafed plant other than grasses and ferns).

Herbicide: A chemical used for killing or controlling the growth of plants.

Herbivore: An animal that eats plants.

Hyphae: One of the thread-like elements that form the **thallus** of a fungus.

Keystone: A species, group of species, habitats (e.g., dead wood) abiotic factors (i.e., fire) that play a pivotal role in ecosystem processes and upon which a large

GLOSSARY

part of the community depends.

Lateral roots: Those underground roots that are approximately parallel to the ground.

Layering: A form of vegetative reproduction in which an intact branch develops roots as the result of contact with soil or other media.

Leader: The terminal, i.e., topmost shoot on a tree.

Legacy Tree: A superior tree, usually mature or old-growth, that is retained on a site after harvesting natural disturbance to provide a biological legacy.

Limbyness Refers to the number of branches or boughs on a tree's stem.

Mixedwood stand: Contains 26 – 75% softwood.

Mutualism: An interaction between the individuals of two or more species in which the growth, growth rate, or population size of both are increased in a reciprocally beneficial association.

Mycelia: The vegetative part of a fungus, composed of **hyahae** and forming a **thallus**.

Mycorrhizae: The usually symbiotic association between higher plant roots and mycelia of specific fungi that aid plants in the uptake of water and certain nutrients and may offer protection against other soil-borne organisms

Nest: A structure or place used by birds for laying eggs and rearing young.

Old growth: The late successional stage of forest development.

Overstory: That portion of trees forming the upper canopy in a stand.

Pace: Two steps equals one pace; used as a unit for measuring approximate distance.

Partial cut: The removal of only part of a stand for purposes other than regenerating a new age class.

Pathogen: A parasitic organism directly capable of causing disease.

Photosynthesize: The manufacturer of organic compounds, particularly carbohydrates in the leaves and needles of plants from carbon dioxide, water, and enzymes in the presence of light as the energy source.

Pioneer: Any new arrival in the early stages of succession.

Pith: The central core of a stem representing the first years of growth and consisting mainly of soft tissue.

Plimsoll line: A mark or line painted on a ship's hull to show how heavily it may be loaded.

Predator: An organism that feeds externally on other organisms.

Primary succession: This occurs on sites that have not previously borne vegetation.

Regenerate: The act of renewing tree cover by establishing new trees naturally or by planting.

Regeneration: Seedlings or **saplings**.

Regime: The characteristic frequency and extent of disturbance within an ecosystem.

Release: A treatment that frees young trees from undesirable, usually overtopping, competing vegetation.

Resilience: The capacity of a community or ecosystem to maintain or regain normal function and development following a disturbance.

Ribes: A group of plants belonging to the Saxifrage family. Includes skunk current, gooseberry, black currant, and red currant.

Riparian: Related to, living, or located in conjunction with a wetland, on the bank of a river or stream but also at the edge of a lake or tidewater.

Root collar: The location of a plant where the vascular anatomy changes from that of a stem to that of a root.

GLOSSARY

Root sucker: Shoot growth from a dormant bud located on a shallow root of a tree.

Rooting depth: The soil found between the duff layer and the "C" horizon that can be occupied by roots.

Rotation: In even-aged stands, the period between regeneration establishment and final harvest.

Rubes: A group of plants belonging to the rose family. Includes wild rose, red raspberry, thimbleberry, and dwarf raspberry.

Sapling(s): A usually young tree larger than a seedling but smaller than a pole.

Secondary Succession: This occurs after the whole or part of the vegetation has been removed.

Selection Management: This type of management regenerates and maintains a multiaged structure by removing some trees in all size classes either singly, in small groups, or in strips.

Self thinning: Within fully-stocked, even-aged stands some individual trees exert dominance while others fall behind and are eventually suppressed and die.

Sere: One part of the successional continuum (i.e., pioneer sere).

Severity: A deep-burning fire.

Shade intolerant: Having the capacity to compete for survival under direct sunlight conditions.

Shade tolerant: Trees which can persist and grow (perhaps slowly) under the shade of other trees.

Shelterwood: The cutting and removal of many trees in a stand, leaving those needed to produce sufficient shade to produce a new age class in a moderated microenvironment.

Shifting mosaic: At any one point in time species composition may change at any specific place on the ground. But on a landscape scale species composition remains relatively constant.

Silviculture: The art and science of controlling the establishment, growth, composition, health, and quality of forests and woodlands to meet the diverse needs and values of landowners and society on a sustainable basis.

Sinker roots: A root other than a tap root that grows straight downward.

Slash: The residue, i.e., tree tops, branches, culls, and knocked down trees left on the ground after logging.

Snag: A standing dead tree.

Softwood stand: Contains 76 – 100% softwood.

Soil texture: The amount of sand, silt and clay in a soil.

Spacing: Also called "cleaning" is a release treatment in an age class not past the sapling stage to free the favored trees from less desirable individuals of the same age class that overtop them or are likely to do so.

Species: The narrowest major category in the classification of plants and animals.

Spring: A small stream of water flowing naturally from the Earth.

Stand: In *ecology*, a contiguous group of similar plants. In *silviculture*, a contiguous group of trees sufficiently uniform in age-class distribution, composition, and structure, and growing on a site of sufficiently uniform quality, to be a distinguishable unit.

Stand type: A class of stand defined for silvicultural or management purposes, usually according to species composition, structure, and age.

Stem damage: Damage such as logging or fire scars, woodpecker holes, animal chews, etc.
Stem snap: Trees broken off by the wind.
Stocking: The number of trees per unit area compared with the desired number for best growth and management. Usually expressed as a percent i.e., 70% stocked.
Stratification: The exposure of seed to a cold, moist treatment to overcome **dormancy** and promote regeneration.
Stump sprout: Regeneration of shoot growth from either adventitious or dormant buds from a cut tree stump.
Substrate: That which is laid or spread under an underlying layer such as subsoil.
Succession: A gradual supplanting of one community of plants by another.
Taper The decrease in diameter of a tree or log from the base upwards or from the larger diameter end to the smaller diameter end in logs.
Thallus: A vegetative, often flattened structure not differentiated into stem, leaves and root. Note: a tallus forms the main body of lichens, liverwort, and fungi.
Thinning: A cultural treatment made to reduce stand density of trees primarily to improve growth.
Topography: The surface features of an area usually described as flat, mound and pit, rolling, hilly, steep, etc.
Truncate: Shortened by cutting off.
Understory: That portion of the trees forming the upper canopy or **overstory**.
Uneven-aged stand: A stand with trees of three or more distinct age classes, either intimately mixed or in small groups.
Viability: The capacity of a seed, spore or pollen grain to

                germinate and develop under given conditions.
Vigor: A flourishing physical condition.
Windthrow: Tree or trees tipped over by wind.